Untie the Knots

Untie the Knots

Untie the knot, let your imagination run wild and weave your stories

The Yarn Weavers

Published 2024 by Collimost Books, Carlisle, CA2 4DH, UK collimostbooks.co.uk

Copyright © The Yarn Weavers 2024

The moral right of the authors of The Yarn Weavers collective to be identified as the author of this work is asserted in accordance with the Copyright, Designs and Patents Act of 1988.

All rights reserved. No part of this publication may be reproduced, distributed, or transmitted in any form or by any means, including photocopying, recording, or other electronic or mechanical methods, without the prior written permission of the publisher, except as permitted by UK copyright law. For permission requests, contact the publisher.

Book Cover by Dave Collier and Lynda Abenchiker.

ISBN 9798340235213

Typeset in Silva Book.

Printed by Amazon KDP.

Dedicated to all who support those in need

Contents

'MUMMY'	1
FORBIDDEN FRUIT – Take 1	6
FIRST FLOOR FLAT	9
A CAT'S TALE	12
DON'T WORRY	16
THE LAST OF THE PAPER	19
A WALK IN THE FOREST	22
A LOST ITEM	26
ISHWARI AND THE HEAVY WEIGHT	30
THE ALARM CLOCK	37
MOONLIGHT SONATA WITH A SIDE OF VEGETABLE SOUP	42
HOW DID THAT HAPPEN?	46
FORBIDDEN FRUIT – Take 2	49
THE LONELY STRANGER	52
THE CHRISTMAS PRESENT	57
MEMORIES	61
SKIN	65
HOME	69
THE STORY COLLECTOR	72
MOVING ON	76
THE MEAT PRODUCERS	80
THE OAK TREE	83

LIFE IS A LOTTERY	87
ONE ARABIAN NIGHT	90
CAROLINE VISITS MARRAKECH	94
THE VOICE	101
LEICESTER SQUARE	105
WAS THAT REALLY ME?	108
CECILIA	111
THE ZOO	118
A DAY IN THE LIFE	122
ONE SCAMMER'S PAYBACK	126
THE DIARY	134
DOORS	137
THROUGH THE WINDOW	141
THE CLOCK STOPPED	144
THE UNPAID BILL	147

PREFACE

The Yarn Weavers are a group of women writers based in Southampton, England, formed by Lynda Abenchiker after she returned to the UK from eight years living in a small town in Spain and realising that, although she was very content, her brain was turning to mulch – there just wasn't enough to challenge it.

> 'Since Covid many groups have floundered and we lost a couple of members, but luckily our stalwart four have kept going.'

Author Lynda Abenchiker:

> I was born in Ilfracombe where I lived until I moved to Canterbury to go to teachers training college. I taught for my entire career, infants, juniors and EFL to both children and adults; as an EFL teacher I worked in many countries including Colombia and Morocco. Independent travel has always been my passion and many of my stories take flavours from different cultures I have lived or travelled in. I started the writing group when I moved back from living in Spain.

Author Bryony A:

> I was born in Southampton and have lived here most of my life. When my children started school I worked in the Civil Service until my retirement in 2005. Since then I have travelled widely with my husband and have been involved in various social groups. I started writing short stories when a poster for a local writing group caught my eye. I enjoy creating the characters and plots for the stories and value the supportive interaction with the other members of the group.

Author Linda H

> I was born in Scotland, and moved to Southampton in 2010 with my job at the time. I then met my husband, and decided to move to Southampton permanently. I have since retired and enjoy attending the writing group, and writing short stories.

Author Mary M

> I was born in Winchester, brought up in rural north Hampshire, and moved to Southampton in the early 1970s. During 1974 I made the decision to fulfil a dream to live and work in Australia spending some five years there, working in office environments.
>
> After my return I stayed with what I knew best, the office world eventually spending 30 years with Hampshire County Council and have been happily retired since December 2013.

All proceeds from sales of the book are donated to local charities, see web page for links to charities supported:

sites.google.com/view/yarnweavers

'MUMMY'

Lynda A

Mummy Found On Building Site

A mummy of indeterminate age has been discovered on a building site in southern Spain.

It was revealed by workmen digging the foundations for a new luxury hotel which is to be built on the formerly undeveloped beach of Santa Ursula.

(This area was previously polluted by a sewage outflow into the sea and considered unsafe for bathing, but it has since been cleaned up according to EU directives.)

All work on the site has been suspended whilst archaeologists determine the age and provenance of the mummy.

It is thought possible that the mummy might indicate remains of an age and civilization undiscovered until now, and experts from all over the world are descending on the site.

The wedding was called off.

He cancelled it two weeks before the big occasion.

All the wedding presents had to be sent back, and all the guests informed of her embarrassment.

He couldn't really explain why he didn't want to marry her. He said the usual things like, 'I'm not old enough to be tied down', 'I think I need to go away and find myself', and 'I'm not good enough for you. This way you are free to go and find someone who will give you the kind of love you deserve'.

But she knew the real reason . . . She knew it was because of her cellulite.

How could anyone love a woman with that thick, blobby, orange-peel skin on her bum and thighs?

He had already left the country, had escaped to Thailand where he felt 'himself' might just be. He had left her with the tickets to their honeymoon destination, and rather than face the pitying looks of their friends, she decided to go ahead and have a break from her public humiliation.

Mummy Exposed

Tomorrow the contents of the mummy found earlier this week on Santa Ursula beach will be exposed as archaeologists cut open the coating.

Precision cutting equipment has been flown out to Spain from the Harvard University Archaeological Department in preparation for this task.

This is necessary as the shell, although rigid, is thought to be a relatively thin veneer; therefore the specialists carrying out the operation will need to be extremely careful in order to ensure that no damage will be inflicted on the contents.

She had alerted her honeymoon destination hotel of the abandonment of her marriage, and asked that no mention be made of this during her visit. The hotel administration showed great sensitivity in sending a taxi to the airport for her rather than impose travel on the coach with the other blissful newlyweds.

In addition they changed her room for a small cottage in the hotel grounds and offered free room service should she require it.

Before she left her mother had given the usual maternal advice.

'Don't go sunbathing mad, you know all about the cancer scares involved with staying too long in the hot sun.'

'Don't forget with the hole in the ozone layer, the sun's rays are much stronger and more likely to burn you, and I think the hole is bigger over that area of the continent.'

'Don't forget, with your obsession about your cellulite, if you get brown on your exposed parts it will emphasise the whiteness of that area that is covered.'

'I've bought you a big bottle of suntan cream. Make sure you put it on every day.'

In her misery she hadn't really thought about such mundane things and was quite pleased with her mother's donation. She had intended to spend as much time on the beach as possible, away from other people, to lick her wounds in peace. She had also decided that she wanted to return home looking relaxed and happy, with a tan that would change the emotions of her friends from pity to envy.

She arrived at her hotel late at night and went straight to bed, travelling had exhausted her.

But she had trouble sleeping. The chorus of the local cicadas had kept her awake; that and the blocked nose as she cried at the disappointment of being here alone instead of with her new husband.

The following day, after breakfasting on the veranda of her little cottage, she put on her new swimsuit and sarong, put her book, towel, suntan cream and water into her beach bag, and set off to find a quiet spot to sunbathe; the beaches near the hotel were full of couples and families; she couldn't deal with that scene yet.

She walked for nearly an hour before she found a tiny deserted cove.

The water looked a little grubby, but that was irrelevant; being a weak swimmer she would not have dared to swim alone.

She took off her sarong and had a furtive look around.

There was no one else in sight, and she felt quite sure that other tourists would not venture so far from the hotel.

She took off her swimsuit.

Yes, she took off her swimsuit! She who had never even sunbathed topless before stripped down to the buff. Well, how else was she to camouflage the cellulite on her lower regions?

Rather than burn, she sensibly gave her whole body a liberal coating of the suntan cream her mother had so thoughtfully provided. Then she lay down on the warmest of sands, closed her eyes, and owing to the paucity of sleep the previous night, was soon dead to the world.

She later awoke, drank a little of her water and turned over to toast her back. In almost an instant she was again comatose.

She never noticed, in her somnolence, how windy it was.

Archaeological Disappointment

Archaeologists today confirmed that the 'mummy' found on Santa Ursula beach in Spain, is not what they had expected or indeed hoped for.

Instead of being the remains of an ancient civilization, it is in fact the body of a comparatively recently deceased young lady.

The body was unclothed, but the police forensic department have found no signs of sexual interference.

Anyone with any knowledge of a young woman who has gone missing in mysterious circumstances in the last ten years is invited to get in touch with the local police to help with their enquiries into this baffling case.

Her disappearance had been reported to the police, but at that time the mayor of the town had just been accused of money laundering, the town hall was on the verge of bankruptcy, and the local police was in disarray.

Her mother, who was never the brightest of women, just thought, 'Oh, she'll come home when she's hungry', (forgetting that her daughter was no longer a child). Besides which, she had allowed her estranged husband to go back to the marital home. He had returned to his old habits of drinking heavily and beating her, so she had problems of her own.

But how had it happened?

Windy conditions had soon covered her in sand, which clung to the liberal coating of suntan cream. This created a casing which was rapidly baked hard by the heat of the midday sun. Nothing could permeate this shell, neither air nor water.

She had suffocated.

Years of sand movement and tides did not disturb her cocoon, just buried it deeper and deeper to be discovered on that fateful day by a digger.

Scientists are now looking into future uses of a mixture that is so impervious to the elements.

FORBIDDEN FRUIT – Take 1

Bryony

Sometimes it is hard to resist the temptation to pluck a forbidden fruit from the tree of life. But beware – once picked it cannot be returned to the tree.

The building had collapsed on top of her but metal girders from the structure had come together to form a sort of arch under which she was sheltered. It was hot and stuffy, and the acrid smell was overpowering. As she recovered consciousness Gina was in a state of shock and disbelief. She had been in the local hospital where she had given birth to a daughter minutes before the earthquake struck. Suddenly her mind cleared and she looked around her for the child. Where was she? Please let her be alive. Gina gasped as she saw a small arm protruding from a pile of rubble a few yards away. But she could not reach the child as her way was blocked by an overturned bed and beams. Slowly she inched her way forward crawling under and around the bed. Carefully removing the rubble, she uncovered the child and clasped it to her. It was female and cold. She examined the child more closely and saw the name tag that the nurse had put around her daughter's wrist. She screamed and fell into a spasm of grief and disbelief.

Then from behind her Gina heard a woman crying and turned around. She called out to her but there was no response. Carefully laying her child's body on the ground Gina made her way towards the sound. After clambering over stones and rubble, and slowly moving forward, she came upon the young girl who had been in the bed beside her in the maternity ward before she was taken into the delivery room. She had confided in Gina that she was not married and that she was worried whether the father of the child would support her. The girl was trapped under a girder with the full weight on her chest. Gina could see that her injuries were very bad. She stroked the girl's forehead to comfort her but although she was moaning incoherently she seemed unaware of Gina's presence.

Gina started shouting for help but nobody responded. Hours passed and the dust and the heat were unbearable. Any light that had first permeated the ruin was fast fading as night fell.

The girl started screaming – a different sort of sound. Gina suddenly felt a rush of warm fluid as the girl's waters broke. What to do – she had never delivered a baby before. The hours passed and the girl's contractions increased. She gave a final loud cry and into this living hell a child was born. As it was still dark all that Gina could do was gather the child to her to keep it warm with the umbilical cord still attached. Eventually she slept cradling the child in her arms.

After a few hours, it started to get light and Gina could feel the child moving in her arms. She automatically put it to her breast where it suckled. Gina could see that it was a boy. She spoke to the girl telling her that she had a lovely son but there was no response. She inched forward to show her the child but she was met by eyes that stared without seeing. Gina knew that she had do something about the umbilical cord that kept the child attached to her mother. There was nothing sharp nearby to enable her to cut the cord so she braced herself and bit through it – then bound it to the child's stomach with a strip torn from her nightdress.

Later Gina heard the sound of voices above her and knocking. She called out to let them know where she was. She told them that she had given birth to a son and that the child was alive. She also told them that there was another female down there with her who was dead with her baby daughter. Gina gently laid the boy on his mother's stomach and crawled back to her own child. She lifted her to her breast and kissed her head with tears pouring down her cheeks then clambered back with her to the dead girl. She placed her beside the girl but first removed the name tag and pushed it under some rubble.

Eventually the searchers were able to reach Gina and she was rescued with the boy child and taken to a waiting ambulance. As they pulled away to be taken to hospital she saw the bodies of the girl and her own daughter being brought to the surface. Then she saw a young man rush forward to the bodies and fall upon them weeping.

For a fleeting moment Gina felt guilty for the swapping the babies but she quickly dismissed the thought. After all the man was still young and could have many other children. But she was a widow – her husband having died a few months previously. The pregnancy had been a surprise as they had been trying unsuccessfully for years – so it had been her last chance. But the baby boy that she held so tightly to her would now belong to her forever.

You may think that Gina should have given the boy child to his father – but having taken the forbidden fruit from the tree she was unable to put it back again without revealing her lies and suffering the consequences. So she said nothing.

FIRST FLOOR FLAT

Linda H

Outside is bleak.

Inside is quiet, except for the soft hum of my laptop. And the silence: silence has a hum all of its own.

I stare through the window again but I'm not sure what I'm hoping to see. There is no activity below in the street. Southampton is a ghost town. A zombie town. A lockdown town.

I go back to my computer; my next Zoom appointment is in half an hour; it's David. I have to talk to him about how he's tried to find work over the last four weeks, as I'm his work coach. It will no doubt be a short meeting.

I am employed by Jobcentre Plus. Our team helps to provide employers with the candidates that are right for them. We also work closely with jobseekers on our books to help them into work.

I go over to my armchair and stare at the mantelpiece. There's a photo of me with Jim and the boys from years ago, before Jim passed away and the boys both married and moved away. I pick it up and run a finger over their faces, over the layer of dust. I haven't seen James and Kevin since March.

After three years I'd been coping pretty well with my grief; it never goes away but it had been a lot gentler and easier, and my day to day life had been good . . . until lockdown.

What I hadn't realised was just how much being busy with work; getting out and about; meeting up with people for meals and outings; travelling; looking after my grandchildren, was enabling me to cope with my grief for Jim.

Now I'm home alone, working from home, only connecting with people by phone or email or Zoom, with loads of time to fill, and I've had time to think again about how I can survive with a Jim-shaped hole in my heart. I have to admit that I really struggled during the first couple of weeks, and became very depressed, but I've worked through that and am in a much better place now.

I think about making a cup of tea, but decide that I will have one later. I sit in the armchair and the sagging cushions arrange themselves around me. I close my eyes, put a thumb and forefinger between them and press hard. It offers no relief.

I'm distracted, when there's a scratching sound, spiked claws against the upholstery of the armchair. It's Felix, he's revving up to ask for food again. I bend over and rub the fur between his ears, and the softness of it makes me breathe out. I shouldn't have brought him home: a kitten contained in a first floor flat isn't really fair.

He springs up on my knee and nuzzles my hand, bumps against it with his wet nose, then he rolls over. It's the exposed belly that does it: utter trust. The legs lifted wide; the rounded hump, black and white, lightly furred. His eyes are almost closed; there's the edge of a fang, the hint of pinkness inside his mouth, I place a hand over his tummy and my palm fits perfectly. He doesn't move; he is purring, waiting, sure that I will feed him.

I press a finger beneath his soft chin and suddenly my face is wet. I swallow the sadness that constricts my throat, the realisation that I've only spoken to three people today, and they were all on Zoom and that I haven't had any human contact for weeks. Just then Felix waves a leg, curls the tip of his tail: he seems to know.

I wipe my eyes on the sleeve of my jumper and pick him up, holding him against my cheek, then I place him on the carpet. He's off, running between my feet, bumping against my ankles as we rush to the kitchen and I throw a few rattling biscuits into a cat bowl.

He's purring again, a little motorised sound of contentment. I decide I'll make a cup of tea after all, then I go back to the computer. David will be on the screen soon to tell me how he tried unsuccessfully to get a job at Costa Coffee. I'll need to sound optimistic!

A CAT'S TALE

Mary

Something is happening. Something is definitely happening because my person is all twitchy. She went up that odd set of steps into the mysterious room in the roof, the one I just haven't been able to get into to explore and she came back with the strange box on wheels that she takes with her when she leaves me in that horrible place in a tiny pen surrounded by other miserable stressed moggies. She also came back with the basket that she puts me in to take me to that place and also uses to take me to the vet where a person in a white coat pokes things into unmentionable places, jabs sharp things into me, looks in my ears and forces me to open my mouth to look at my teeth. I just want to bite them then they would know there was nothing wrong with my teeth. I know that basket means trouble, usually for me. Does she think I am stupid?

She has taken the box on wheels into her bedroom, I'm not allowed in there. Now I am even more convinced she is going somewhere. The basket, which is always referred to as my basket, has disappeared into the library room, I'm not allowed in there either but that doesn't bother me as there is nowhere soft or comfortable to sleep.

Now what? Oh no, that noisy machine she pushes up and down the carpet is coming out of its cupboard. That's it, this is just too much I'm off to hide in the garden.

I'm not sure how long I have been outside, I must have fallen asleep in my favourite warm shady spot but I can now hear her voice and the rattling of my favourite treats box, it must be tea time. I tell myself to proceed with caution as this may be a trap to get me into that basket. As I trot, do cats do that? I thought it was something horses did, no matter. As I trot down the garden towards the house I see she has someone with her whom I vaguely recognise, ah yes, I remember now it's her friend who comes to stay when she and my person spend hours sorting through hundreds of apples to find four the same size. I have yet to figure out why! But there are no apples now so why is she here?

I meow piteously as they get my tea. Honestly how long does it take to open the pouches? It's not as if they have to cook it, someone has already done that. Don't they realise how hungry I am, it is very demanding sleeping most of the day. No sign of my basket so not a trap then. My basket! I ask you, as if I would want such a thing. After tea I settle down for a well-earned sleep in the rocking chair by the window in the lounge. All too soon it is time for me to move into my bed in the kitchen for an uneventful night but I am locked in as usual.

The next morning my person is up very early and has the box on wheels with her. The friend wanders downstairs and they both sit in the dining room for a while until my person puts on her coat and leaves with the box on wheels. It would seem that I am not going to the horrible place to stay in the tiny pen but am to stay at home and be looked after by the friend. I don't know the friend very well but she seems nice enough.

Did I say nice? I don't think so, she tried to brush me and I wasn't having any of that. I hissed, I spat and I tried, unsuccessfully, to bite her. I turned into a black ball of hissing spitting furry fury then I ran off into the garden and glared out from under the patio chairs. Thank goodness she had given me my breakfast first because there was no way I was going back into that kitchen for it.

It has been a lovely day, I stayed out all day but I'm hungry again now so I will have to be brave and go in for my tea. She is talking to someone who isn't there. I think she has one of those things called a mobile phone. My person doesn't have one. She's talking about someone or something called Sid Vicious. She says bye and wanders into the kitchen and is talking to me but why is she calling me Sid? My name is not Sid.

Think I'll lull her into false sense of security and spend the evening sitting on her lap. She's just got a drink and settled down in my person's seat in front of that thing that sometimes has moving pictures and speaks. Here goes, I jump up and settle down. Actually this is quite comfy and she's not calling me Sid but my proper name so she must have forgiven me for my outburst of bad temper this morning but it was her own fault.

Just had a thought, I know what I can do to cause maximum stress and worry – it is such a lovely warm night I'll stay out all night. Must make sure she can see me in the garden and I will ignore her when she calls or comes out with my favourite treats, it will be hard to resist the temptation of the treats but needs must. Well that went better than I expected, think I might do that again. She was really stressed and out looking for me every two hours or so setting off the floodlights in the garden which will properly annoy the neighbours as they take ages to shut off. The sun is shining now so think I'll have a snooze in another of my favourite spots under the summerhouse then go in for breakfast.

As I come in through my special door I meow piteously all the way into the kitchen and then meow even louder when I see she hasn't even started to get my breakfast. She makes a fuss of me and suddenly I feel something wet on the nape of my neck, oh yuk, it's my flea treatment. Normally I would disappear rapidly and sulk in the garden but I want my breakfast so I pretend not to notice.

I did stay out for another night but it didn't have the same impact as she went to bed and ignored the fact that I wasn't inside so won't bother again. The next few days passed as usual for me, a round of eating and sleeping and before I know it my person is back with the box on wheels and the friend disappears with another box on wheels. I didn't know she had one as I was in the garden when she arrived. The garden is my favourite place in the whole world unless it is raining then I like to be sleeping on the rocking chair in the lounge.

DON'T WORRY

Lynda A

Either Edward really, deeply loved me, or he was incredibly lazy and laid back . . . lacking the energy to make a change in what was a relatively undemanding and comfortable lifestyle.

His response to all the upsets in our life was, 'Don't you worry, it's not important' . . . anything from burning the dinner (he said he liked his food nicely browned) to the time I left the bath water running whilst chatting on the phone and flooded the house. Each time he would find an excuse for me . . . the cooker was on the blink, the water pressure was erratic etc.

I wrote off the car once by driving over a raised roundabout whilst in a drunken stupor one night. Any other man would at least have raised his voice, but not my Edward. He merely patted my hand, told me not to worry, how he had always said it was a silly place to put a roundabout. He then quietly and calmly phoned the garage and arranged to have the car taken away and disposed of. From then on he had to go to work by bike, but he reassured me that it wasn't important, that the bike ride was better for his health and would probably help to ease the arthritis that occasionally caused him crippling pain in his hips.

After many years of such gently resigned reaction to life's crises, it came as no surprise to me that he didn't get upset when I killed his mother with a carving knife one Sunday lunch. He stroked my back and calmed me, saying she should never have accused me of making lumpy gravy. Then, in his usual tranquil fashion, he put the knife in the sink, dragged his mother's body into the downstairs bath (which we had luckily had put in after the previous disaster) and hacked her into manageable size portions with his chainsaw. He popped each portion into a Tesco's bag and tied the top. He then filled black bin liners with these individual packs interspaced with wodges of newspaper. 'Don't you worry', he said to me, 'The tip will be open in the morning . . . these won't get under your feet for long'. By the time he had meticulously cleaned the bath, his saw and the carving knife, the pudding was ready to be served up, and there was enough for two helpings each.

His kindness to me was a great relief when unbelievable tragedy struck.

I had been in town shopping all day and my feet felt strange, a discomfort I'd never experienced before. When I took my shoes off I could see the reason. Since leaving home that morning, my toenails had grown about an inch; the pressure had caused the discomfort. A footbath and nail-clip remedied it for that day.

The following morning I found they had grown a further two inches overnight. This was very strange, but again I dealt with them and got on with my daily chores.

This strange phenomenon accelerated at an incredible rate. Within a week my toenails were growing about an inch an hour. We called the doctor who suggested I stop taking HRT, cut back on my calcium intake and barred anything with gelatine from my diet. He admitted that he had never encountered anything like this before, that he would look it up on the internet and get back to me if he found anything. I never heard from him again, but followed his instructions to the letter.

My toenails were changing. They were no longer shell-like appendages to my toes, they sprouted out gnarled and twisted; they corkscrewed out like roots in a mangrove swamp. The faster their growth, the thicker and harder they became.

I hadn't the strength to cut them so hard had they become; Edward had to carry out this chore for me with a pair of tin snips. He had to trim them on waking, before lunch, after tea and before going to bed. I found this undignified, but he would reassure me with his, 'Don't worry, it's not that important in the grand scheme of things'.

He kept his stoical attitude when forced to sleep on the sofa as my nails were causing lacerations to his legs in our shared bed where the sheets were getting more shredded nightly.

As my toenails grew thicker and thicker, harder and harder, so they seemed to leach the strength from the bones in my body. As those nails grew so my bones shrank, leaving me a couple of inches shorter by the day. The excess skin left by this shrinkage I tucked into the track suit bottoms I had taken to wearing now I was housebound.

In less than a month I had shrivelled to the size of a child and could see no end to it. Very soon my toenails would be the death of me. The skeleton that had once supported my body would have completely disappeared through the ends of my toes, leaving just a pile of useless skin and flesh.

I can imagine Edward when that time comes. He will meticulously fold me up and pop me into a shoe box. 'Don't you worry', I can hear him say, 'It's not important, I'll get this sorted out'. And I can imagine him calmly digging a hole in the back garden and burying the shoe box next to the hamster and the goldfish. Quite reassuring really.

THE LAST OF THE PAPER

Bryony

It was the last of the paper that she had managed to smuggle into prison in her bodice so Françoise decided to write for the final time to her dear friends.

My dearest friends,

I am sorry that this letter will be so short but I have only one sheet of paper left as Papa has used the rest to plead our case.

I did not want to go without saying goodbye to you both and to tell you how much you mean to me. Our jailer has agreed to pass the letter to someone he says he trusts after I have gone to meet with Madame Guillotine – so I hope that he does not let me down as it has cost me dearly.

My dear Louise – so pretty and petite. I am so glad that you managed to escape to England as I fear that you would have been much abused if you had been here. Even with my plain countenance I have had to endure much humiliation from the jailers, and you are so much lovelier than me. You were always so kind, caring and thoughtful, and I thank you from the bottom of my heart for all that you did for everyone – especially the children.

My dear Thérèse – thank you for taking Louise with you even though she wanted to stay and hide. You were so brave crossing through the woods that dark night and then being hidden under the waste from the chateau in the wagon before reaching the boat. It must have smelled so foul and been so cold – so I'm glad that Louise had you to cling to. You always were the one who sorted things out and encouraged us to be adventurous. Our lives would have been less fulfilling without you.

I do not know when it will be our turn to travel in the tumbril to the square where the guillotine stands, but I do not think that it will be long now as the other cells are emptying quickly. I have been giving my meagre food rations to the children so at least they will not feel so hungry when they make their last journey. How tragic that their lives will be ended before they have hardly begun. Papa says that he will smother them in their sleep rather than let them die that way but I'm not sure that Mama will agree. But as I know so little about the ways of death I am not in a position to judge what would be the least painful and traumatic way to go. But I think that Papa may be right?

I only hope that God gives me the courage to die with dignity. It is rumoured that some have to be bound and manhandled before they meet their end screaming in terror and begging for mercy. It is said that the spectators have no pity and cheer each time the blade falls. I try not to think too much about it but I hope that it is a quick end.

So my dearest friends please pray for me and keep me safe in your memory for my only crime was my status at birth. And even though many have testified at the tribunal trial that our family was kind to our servants and tenants, and made provision for their welfare – we have all been found guilty and condemned to death.

My blessings to you both and Adieu.
Your ever loving friend Françoise.

The letter never reached the intended recipients as despite having used Françoise most despicably, and promised to take the letter outside the prison to be given to someone who knew how to get it delivered – the jailer just tore it up and put it in his brazier as he had done previously with all the other letters entrusted to him. But at least Françoise died thinking that her friends would receive it so that was one small mercy.

A WALK IN THE FOREST

Linda H

I had spent years thinking about getting a dog. Unfortunately, my very demanding job; long working day and my tiny second-floor flat made it an impossible dream.

However, in the summer of 2019 my life began to change. Firstly I was left an inheritance, which allowed me to move from my tiny flat into a ground floor flat with a garden. Then I was offered early retirement. My company were taken over by new American owners, and were downsizing staff numbers. This came with a very generous financial package, which, if I budgeted carefully, would allow me to have a good standard of living.

I could finally have time for myself to read more; take up some new hobbies and most importantly – get a pet.

After that things moved very quickly. By autumn I was settled into my new flat; I was now retired and was the owner of a very cute rescue dog. Barney was a spaniel/terrier cross, just the ideal size and temperament for me to manage. My flat was close to several parks and only ten minutes drive to the New Forest, so Barney and I spent the next few months getting to know each other and going for long walks in the forest. One of my retirement presents had been a new camera. I would take this with me and stop every so often to snap away, while Barney ran ahead.

We both loved our walks in the forest. I admired the beauty of the woods that surrounded me. If it was sunny, the treetops created a canopy over my head. As autumn progressed, the crimson and auburn foliage was a magnificent sight. The leaves appeared as though they were dying to fall out of the trees and join the others on the forest floor.

As autumn turned to winter, the wind created the sound of rustling leaves. Together with the other flora, the leaves formed a thick springy carpet for me to walk on. Along the way, fallen branches accompanied the thickets of weeds.

Then as Christmas approached, we began taking longer walks, as we were now comfortable with each other. Barney trusted me not to leave him. He would wander ahead of me but always came when he was called. On our longer walks, I would often stop to take photographs. Then I would have a drink of coffee from my flask and Barney would have a drink of water from his portable bowl. We would rest underneath the shade of the trees and I could smell the scent of pine needles, the very ambience of Christmas. Occasionally a red-breasted robin would appear. One day, a single sparrow fluttered high above and small animals scampered around.

So, as well as all the exercise, I was taking many lovely photos and Barney was also getting plenty of exercise, as he ran off, chasing rabbits and smelling old leaves.

We had a very enjoyable and busy few months. I had retired from work, but not from life. At my leaving party a wise friend told me, 'Don't be afraid to make this phase of your life the most memorable'.

As we went into the new year, 2020, the weather was terrible and our walks in the forest became less frequent. We had to make do with the local park. By the beginning of March we were missing our long walks, so we drove out to the New Forest a few times. We didn't realise that those would be our last outings for a long time.

By the end of March the whole country was in lockdown. I couldn't believe how quickly we all got used to something you would never imagine being normal. Not at first – of course there was that strange period of adjustment; that unreal feeling; the silence; the quietness. It was all so surreal, the daily briefing, the feeling of quiet camaraderie; we were all in this together.

After the first few weeks of isolating, a routine built up, and in some strange way, became our new way of life.

I still took Barney for his daily walks, but they were shorter and more local. No drives out to the New Forest. All around, the streets were deserted, apocalyptic, with queues of people waiting to get into the shops, all at an orderly two metres apart. The masks became commonplace.

If someone had told me in 2019, that by the following year we would be living like this, each in our own sterilised anti-bac world, I would never have believed them. Slowly, hesitantly, almost as though they'd forgotten how to do it, everyone came out to their doors every Thursday at 8pm. Like everything else it soon became a part of our new life. We would stop what we were doing and clap for the heroes who were out facing an unseen, terrifying, unthinkable battle. A rousing chorus of applause ringing out, echoing far and wide. It was simply beautiful. Every week, before I realised what was happening, the tears would stream down my face.

Slowly, we edged past Easter, and the cherry blossom trees began to bloom and fall, a sure sign that May was on its way. As summer came, the birds emboldened by the quietness of the streets, began to fly around. The neglected verges became jungles of long grasses stretching triffid-like towards the sky. A whole variety of flowers grew in places you wouldn't expect. The flowers continued to bloom vibrantly, although the earth was a little dry as it has been ridiculously hot and rain-free for a British summer.

I felt reassured by the fact that in spite of everything, Mother Nature just kept on going regardless. I found great comfort in that.

Last week was my birthday, July 17th, and the prime Minister gave me a lovely present. He announced plans for a 'significant return to normality'. Already, outside beyond the rooftops, beyond the flats, there are signs of the usual hustle and bustle, the background noise has begun its familiar hum. It's not quite back to normal – it is quieter than before – but tentatively, steadily, life is returning to the streets.

This is the new normal. Whether it is better than the old one still waits to be seen, like everything in life, a story waiting to be told – it's in the hands of people to decide how it unfolds.

But I know that I am now looking forward to 2021, it should all be over by then, and Barney and I can have many more walks in the Forest.

A LOST ITEM

Mary

It was just lying there, a crumpled item on the pavement and could, at first glance, have been anything, a wrapper from a chocolate bar, a crisp packet, a cigarette packet or any one of a hundred types of rubbish discarded in the street by those too lazy and thoughtless to put it in the bin which was only a few feet away.

It caught Jean's eye as she wandered past, she wasn't in a hurry that morning being early for her dental appointment and thinking there were many things she could be doing or places she would rather be than spending time in the dental surgery. It caught her eye as it seemed to be suspended as all the other items of detritus were caught in the eddies caused by passing vehicles and the scurrying hurrying feet of pedestrians on their way to work in one of the many offices and shops in the town.

She picked it up. Closer inspection revealed a cream-coloured envelope still quite clean but rather crumpled. How had it got there? There was obviously something in it as the envelope had weight and even though crumpled there were sharp corners. Jean stuffed it into her coat pocket and went on her way. She didn't want to examine it in the street as she felt that passers-by might look at her with the same pity they reserved for those down on their luck who scoured the pavements for cigarette butts and anything else useful.

The dental treatment was every bit as awful as she had feared, painful and expensive. The vague idea of coffee and cake afterwards, usually a treat, evaporated as she felt she had more than a passing resemblance to a chipmunk. Jean went home where she retrieved the envelope from her pocket before putting her coat away.

The envelope contained a banknote, 1000 somethings from somewhere, she couldn't tell as there didn't appear to be any writing just some symbols that looked like pictures – perhaps they were the writing? Also in the envelope was a postcard-sized sepia coloured picture of a strange-shaped boat with a backdrop of mountains. There were no clues as to where it could be but she had seen similar boats featured in the glossy travel brochures of exotic places that she loved to read knowing that she would never see them. There was one such brochure on the coffee table and there on the front cover was a similar looking vessel so China or Asia she thought. The banknote offered no obvious clues so out came her computer, the one she always said she didn't want and didn't need but now couldn't live without as it kept her in touch with her family scattered across America and Canada.

With the discomfort from the dental work all but forgotten Jean started her quest to track down the origins of the banknote. Hooray for search engines she thought as some while later she was convinced she had identified the note as 1000 Cambodian Riels. The picture held no clues so she assumed the two items belonged together and were from Cambodia.

Jean made a cup of tea which she always found aided her thought process. She turned her attention to the envelope smoothing it out and carefully examining every inch of it. In one corner she found something that appeared to be similar symbols to those on the banknote. If it was Cambodian where was she going to find someone to translate it? Oh come on she thought, she lived in a big busy town where hundreds of people from countries around the world had made their home and brought their cuisine. All she needed to do was find a Cambodian restaurant – simple.

But it wasn't. Computer searches showed only one, a takeaway, in the town and that was in an area with a bad reputation for drug related crime. Jean was determined to

27

solve the mystery of the envelope so she decided to seek out the restaurant that very evening. She put the envelope, banknote and picture separately in her handbag.

It was raining when Jean left, that fine drizzle that soaks you through before you realise – sticky rain she called it. The bus journey was uneventful, a busy rush hour service emptying out passengers at every stop. As the bus neared her destination she realised that there were only four passengers left, three young men in hoodies with the hoods pulled low to hide their faces and herself. The bravado that brought her here evaporated as the bus pulled up outside a small row of unprepossessing shops including the restaurant.

Jean got off the bus, pulling her coat tightly around her as she did so, and approached the restaurant which was brightly lit and appeared clean. Taking a deep breath she pushed the door open, once inside her senses were assailed by delicious aromas and she immediately felt hungry. This is not why you are here she told herself sternly. Two men appeared from the kitchen area of the restaurant, the younger one asking her what she wanted in broken English. She produced the envelope from depths of her bag and handed it to the man asking simply what did it say.

The two men looked at each other, speaking excitedly in their native language and gesticulating wildly. Jean had no idea what was going on but the tone of their voices was not angry. The older man called out loudly and a young woman in her twenties joined them from the kitchen. He handed her the envelope and as he did so explained something, she looked inside and tears filled her dark eyes. She held the envelope out towards Jean almost begging. 'Please', she said her voice thick with tears, her accent heavy. 'Please', she said again. Jean was puzzled, what did she want? Then she realised the young woman was looking for the contents.

Jean again rummaged in her large handbag pulling out the picture and the banknote which she handed to her. A beautiful smile lit the young woman's face, she clasped Jean's hands repeating her thanks several times. In broken English and with many gestures she explained her sister had sent them, but she had been in a hurry just putting them in her pocket and later lost them.

Jean felt very emotional as she left the restaurant, suddenly that painful visit to the dentist took on a rosy glow.

ISHWARI AND THE HEAVY WEIGHT

Lynda A

Word spreads quickly around Badami, our village. It is a small, insular kind of place, consisting of one main street with a few small streets and lanes running at right angles towards the country. Few people ever come to Badami unless to visit family here, and even fewer leave the village. There is a kind of incestuous feeling, in fact many of the families have inbred, and the resultant mutants can be seen wandering the back streets.

Today word has it that an old lady who lived in Alley 3, Ishwari Sidiq by name, has finally left her mortal coil and gone to Paradise.

Ishwari Sidiq and her husband Shebir had been good friends of ours for many years, like us they were good, practising Hindus. We had spent many evenings sitting under the baobab tree in their garden, or under the fig tree in ours, thanking the gods for a good harvest and revelling in the coolness that ushers in the night.

Shebir had been the more garrulous of the two, always knew the latest gossip and was more than happy to share it with anyone who would listen. Ishwari had been an unceasingly good friend to me – a quiet, empathetic and non-judgemental ally when times got bad.

But the closeness had evaporated when Shebir became sick. Till this day I don't know what exactly was wrong with him. At first Ishwari informed me that it was a very contagious illness. Whatever it was, it was certainly debilitating; Shebir became wheelchair bound, he could be seen sitting in his chair by the sitting room window or on the porch, but never again did he venture into the centre or make any attempt to communicate with friends, in fact he shunned any contact. Ishwari once mentioned on one of her rare visits, that he was so disfigured by his illness that he couldn't bear to be seen, he preferred to stay a hermit for the rest of his life than to see the pity in the eyes of his friends at how this mystery illness had affected him.

About six months later, I had tried to visit my good friend Ishwari, but she had not invited me into the house. She had spoken to me through the window, seeming distraught and distracted. She had terminated our conversation abruptly by closing the shutters in my face. I must admit it, I was extremely hurt.

Well, you know how life is, something that really hurts one day fades into insignificance when life throws its other rubbish at you, and somehow I hadn't really kept up with Ishwari and Shebir; our friendship, strong though I thought it had been, had not withstood the rigours of time and life.

So here we were, and I feel ashamed to admit it, twenty years down the line, twenty years of being so totally absorbed in my life and I heard from someone else that Ishwari was dead.

Of course all the women of the village went to their house. The body must be cleaned and laid out. Also the disabled husband must be fed and looked after.

It was with some trepidation that I approached the house of my old friend. I was originally shocked by the state of the garden and exterior of the house, but then none of us are getting any younger and it must have been difficult for Ishwari, trying to keep everything up together all by herself.

As I drew nearer I became aware of a hum of conversation from a large group of women standing outside the house – I couldn't understand what they were doing outside, why were they not inside sorting things out for the couple.

I greeted the women, all of whom I know by name, and we exchanged the usual pleasantries. Once these were out of the way we could get down to the subject of what they were doing outside.

The problem, it turned out, was Shebir.

Ishwari had just passed away from old age and exhaustion. Her body had been found that morning in the garden, she had been cutting back some foliage and had just let go of life. The doctor had been called, written a death certificate, and left it to the women to carry her inside and see to her. They had already dealt with her body, had cleaned it, massaged in the sweet smelling oils we put on our dead and arranged her body ready for her cremation surrounded by garlands of flowers.

Shebir was another matter completely. He was dead too, but they didn't know how he had died, how long he had been deceased, what on earth had gone on in that house. Nobody wanted to go back in – something evil, something unnatural had happened in there; you could feel something noxious in the atmosphere of the house.

I had to go in, I had to experience it for myself; whatever misfortune had befallen my erstwhile friends, it was essential that I try and find out all I could about it.

So I crept into the dark, dank humidity of the house whose shutters had been kept closed for so many years against prying eyes. Once my eyes had become used to the darkness after the brilliance of the sun outside, I could take stock of my bearings. There, on the table in the sitting room lay the prepared body of Ishwari. Seeing her there brought it home how long it had been since our days of closeness; the once abundant black hair lay sparse and grey around her face; a face that had once shone clear and smooth, was now a maze of wrinkles. The reality of the situation brought tears to my eyes, how could I have ignored her for so long? I kissed her gently on the cheek, asking her to accept my apologies and wishing her luck and happiness in the next life.

Then I became aware of another presence in the room, I could feel someone's eyes on me. I turned round quickly and there was

Shebir, sitting as usual in his wheelchair, empty face gazing in my direction. I can tell you now; it gave me quite a start. I went over to where he was and put out my hand to touch his shoulder. I knew he was dead, I knew he probably would not feel like an alive person, but I was not prepared for the way he did feel. I touched his hand and his head and then recoiled in horror. He felt more like a statue than a person. He was not only cold and stiff, which you would expect from a corpse. He was hard – it was like he had a shell.

The more I looked at him, the stranger it all seemed. I went to the window and opened the shutters, I felt it was too eerie to cope with in the dark, but unlike the women outside I felt a need to get to the bottom of this mystery rather than wait outside for the doctor to come back, which could take all day.

The daylight illuminated other factors that added to my bewilderment. Whereas Ishwari's face and hair had shown the passage and ravages of time, Shebir's face was smooth and showed no wrinkles; his hair was still as dark and lustrous as it had been when I last saw him close to – about twenty-one years ago, then it had been slicked down with Brylcream, now it was slicked down with something very hard.

The house had not been thoroughly cleaned for some time, obviously Ishwari had found it all too cumbersome; cobwebs decorated the corners, everything was coated in a layer of gritty dust, including her husband. Thinking of his pride, and how he had always liked to be immaculate, I was tempted to give him a quick once-over with a feather duster; but decided against it in case it was a police matter and I had tampered with the scene of the crime.

I was sorely tempted to go into the bedroom to see if I could find anything else to explain the mystery, but this was not my house and I had to respect their privacy. There was nothing else in the sitting room to help in my quest, so I went outside to wait with the other women until the doctor came.

Luckily it was not a long wait, but it was a futile one.

On hearing our information, Dr Singh went into the house unaccompanied. About ten minutes later he reappeared pushing Shebir in his wheelchair with a blanket draped over his head, he pushed the corpse into the back of the ambulance and left without a word to anyone.

Well, you can imagine, it didn't take long for word to be spread throughout our little village. Everyone was puzzled, but everyone had an opinion about what might have happened in that house. Stories ran from the bizarre to the downright disgusting. Nothing much of great excitement happens in our village and this was obviously going to be the main topic of conversation for some time to come.

It was all too grotesque for my peace of mind. I couldn't eat or sleep after being in that mausoleum of a house and observing the discrepancies within. I had to get to the bottom of this enigma.

After much time spent in deliberation, I decided to visit the Sadhu who had lived in one of the ruined temples behind the village for as many years as I could remember.

I put together an offering of sweet cakes, honey, flowers and perfumed oil for the holy man, and as the heat of the day sent most inhabitants to the sanctuary of their homes, I made my way up to the cliff face where the temples were located.

The Sadhu was in the last temple – its position at the top of two hundred steps and past several troupes of monkeys ensured that he received few visitors and little distraction from his holy meditations.

I arrived hot and exhausted at the entrance to his temple. He invited me to sit and refresh myself with some cool water, saying he had been expecting me. He received my offerings graciously and then asked me to tell him of my preoccupation.

I had wanted to be very calm and quiet in the telling, but somehow as soon as I started recounting the story I became quite distraught and it all came tumbling out in a rush of near-hysteria. He sat very quietly, making no interjections, until I had finished my outpouring.

Only then did he lift his eyes and look at me. Those eyes held all the compassion in the world.

He had known that sooner or later the story would have to come to light. He had hoped it would be later, that his own death would supersede this, and that the mystery would have to remain just that. But then life does not always turn out as we would like it to.

He had received a visit from Ishwari all those many years previously. She had been distraught. Shebir was desperately ill; she felt he was on the brink of death. He was the love of her life; she would never desire another man, she wanted to be with him through Eternity in the next life, BUT . . . and here the Sadhu hesitated, she could not bring herself to jump onto his funeral pyre when he was cremated. How she had cried and torn handfuls of her hair from her scalp. She adored her man, but knew herself to be completely incapable of honouring him in his status as her husband by this final act of subservience.

Although he should have advised her differently according to his position in their religion, he felt a lot of sympathy for this woman who was still young, vital and very afraid. She confessed that although she had given every sign of being a good Hindu wife, of having the same strong beliefs as her husband, she had in fact been brought up as a Catholic. According to these beliefs, if she committed suicide (and jumping onto her husband's funeral pyre would be viewed as such) she would not get to Heaven to spend eternity with her beloved.

The poor soul had been in torment and felt she had no one else to turn to.

He had been obliged to offer her some succour.

He had an acquaintance living in a nearby town who was an embalmer by trade. The only solution he could see was to use the skills of this man to embalm her spouse, then to keep him with her until her own demise.

That is what they had done once Shebir had shuffled off his mortal coil.

Under the guise of taking Shebir on a hospital visit to have tests carried out, they had visited the embalmer. He had agreed to embalm the body using a mixture of formaldehyde and lime that should keep the corpse fresh for longer and inhibit the progress of maggots; but he couldn't predict how long the embalming process would actually offer complete protection, so he suggested putting on a couple of layers of a matt varnish to shield his work.

And so Ishwari had had the sole company of her dead husband for the past twenty years. It was an unimaginable existence.

So now the Sadhu and I must share the story behind this mystery. It is a very heavy mantle to wear.

THE ALARM CLOCK

Bryony

The alarm clock was like an old friend to Fred. Originally it had been white and shiny but was now rather grey and mottled due to its age, and the winder sometimes fell off. It had been with Fred throughout his life – in good times and bad – although like himself it was not as accurate and reliable as it had been – sometimes going off at inconvenient or incorrect times, and often a bit slow. On occasion it stopped altogether and was particularly prone to doing so at 3.35 in the afternoon. This was not a great problem for Fred as it just meant that he woke up later from his nap – but that did not bother him as he was not in a rush to go anywhere! Fred had to admit that both he and the alarm clock were probably coming to the end of their days.

You could almost say that the alarm clock was an antique – indeed he had heard that an item had to be over fifty years old to be classed as such although he did not know whether this was actually the case. He had been given the clock when he was twenty-two and had first left home – and he was now nearing eighty-five. When he had lived with his parents he had not needed an alarm clock as his mother was always an early riser and had woken him with 'a nice cup of tea'. But when he had moved to a small flat in London on promotion he had needed the alarm clock to make sure that he got up in time as he was a deep sleeper and his mother often used to have to shake him before he woke up properly. His parents had bought the alarm clock for him as a going-away present as his mother was worried about him waking up on time. In fact even with the alarm he had nearly been late for work on a couple of occasions until a colleague told him about the trick of placing the alarm in a metal bowl. The first time he had used this method he had woken with such a start that he cricked his neck and suffered with it all day – but he soon got used to it and considered this to be a reliable solution.

When he married Evie the clock had gone with him to the house they rented – although he did not have to use the metal bowl method any more as Evie was a light sleeper and would dig him in the ribs if he did not turn it off. And then it was his job to get up and make the tea which he used to bring back to bed with him so they could drink it together and chat about their plans for the day. After the children arrived – two boys and a girl – the only time that they got tea in bed together was at the weekend as mornings were too busy getting everyone fed and sorted out. But the alarm clock kept going throughout the children's school years and beyond. The alarm clock even used to come on holiday with the family. They generally hired a caravan or sometimes a large tent to stay in either somewhere by the sea or in the countryside. And although the excitement of being on holiday meant that the children were always up at the crack of dawn Fred felt more secure with clock beside him at night. He liked the loud tick of the clock as it soothed him to sleep.

After the children left home Fred and Evie downsized to a smaller house, and Evie said that it was about time that they got a new more modern alarm clock. Fred did not agree as he was fond of the clock but Evie wanted one of those new-fangled *Teasmade* contraptions so they could wake up to a cup of tea without having to get out of bed. In the end she got what she wanted so Fred took the alarm clock down the garden to his little shed so that he could keep an eye on the time when he was in the garden or pottering in the shed. When he retired the shed became his den and he furnished it with an old armchair and a table on which he had a camping stove to make a brew. And if he fancied a nap in the chair in the summer when it was warm enough he used to set the alarm clock to wake him up.

Eventually Evie got fed up with the Teasmade as she said that it was too much bother to set up every night so Fred brought the clock back in from the shed. But by now it was beginning to look its age and was scratched so Evie said that she did not want it in the bedroom as it looked out of place, and bought a clock radio for their bedroom. She put the old alarm clock in a box to go to the church jumble sale but unbeknown to her Fred took it out and put it in the cupboard under the stairs.

When Evie died Fred had felt very lonely. The children all lived some distance away and only visited infrequently – and then only for a few hours at a time as they were busy with their families and careers. Fred was still active so he used to go to the local pub a couple of times a week for a pint and a chat. He also went weekly to a community centre for a cooked lunch for pensioners. It was here that he heard about the new warden-controlled retirement flats that were now ready for occupation with a communal lounge area where the residents could meet and socialise. Fred thought that it sounded ideal and after going to view the show flat he decided to proceed with the purchase. The company arranged everything from selling his old home, legal procedures and advising on de-cluttering his possessions to fit his new flat. They also sorted out the removals for him. Fred realised that it probably would have been cheaper if he had managed it all himself but it was nice to have someone to sort it all out for him as he did not want to bother the family, and did not really feel up to all the organisation himself.

Fred moved in and of course the alarm clock came with him. He had brought it in from the shed after Evie died as the familiar ticking made him feel safe and secure. He had made sure that the de-cluttering did not include the old clock, but he did give it a treat and took it to a watchmaker to get it cleaned and serviced. The watchmaker agreed with Fred that they did not make things as durable as this anymore, although he did persuade him to buy another alarm clock as a spare – just in case.

Fred was very pleased with the small flat as it was compact and it did not take much effort to keep clean and tidy as it had been designed with the elderly in mind. And the alarm clock was back in its rightful place beside his bed once more. Sometimes when Fred could not be bothered to go to the communal lounge – especially if the women had one of their sewing and knitting events – he brought the clock into the living room to keep him company as the ticking was companionable while he was reading a book. Mind you he always made a point of going down after the event had finished as he knew there would be some cake going free. Fred had to admit that the women in the flats did look after him in that respect, but although he liked a nice piece of cake and enjoyed their company there was no one who he had taken a particular shine to – despite a few of them trying to get more cosy with him. As far as he was concerned 'too much water had flowed under the bridge' to make him want to start a new relationship and get used to another woman's ways. Although he did sometimes wish that he had someone to cuddle up to at night to keep his feet warm.

Time passed and Fred began to spend less time downstairs as it really was too much bother to get himself looking presentable, and much easier to stay in his old but comfortable clothes in the flat. The warden in the flats had arranged for him to get ready meals that could be ordered in bulk and kept in the freezer to go into the microwave. Although they were not as tasty as fresh cooked food it certainly made things easier. The warden also ordered Fred's basics like tea, coffee, toiletries and bread online and they got delivered to his door. So there really was no reason to go out and about. But the visits from the family were getting less frequent and sometimes the only contact that he had with them for months was the occasional phone call.

Fred was gradually slowing down in all aspects of his life but overall he was content as he was warm, had plenty to eat, had visits from the other residents who usually brought him cakes if female, and he enjoyed the TV. And of course the old alarm clock was always beside him keeping him company with its regular ticking. Everyone was amazed at how long it had lasted. But one day when the warden went to the flat for her daily visit to check on Fred she found him asleep in his armchair, and noticed that the clock had stopped ticking. As usual the clock showed

3.35, and when she touched Fred's hand she realised that he had stopped ticking too.

The alarm clock was placed beside Fred in his coffin as everyone knew that he would not want to be parted from it – and when the coffin was carried to the hearse it started ticking again on its own as it accompanied Fred on his final journey.

MOONLIGHT SONATA WITH A SIDE OF VEGETABLE SOUP

Linda H

Jamie stared at his wife across the table, noticing for the first time that her jumper was on inside-out. Every morning he would lay out her clothes on the bed in a specific order, so she'd know which item to put on first. But it didn't guarantee how Margaret would put on each item. He would have to pay more attention before they went out in future.

Their usual waitress, Mary, appeared, holding a tray with two mugs of tea on it.

'Hello Mr and Mrs McLean. How are you both today?' She said in her usual friendly way.

With dementia, there were good days and then there were challenging days. Today was one of the latter. Margaret was preoccupied, scratching at a mark on the wooden table, forgetting it was a permanent fixture. They had been lunching at this café once a week, for years now. That scratch had been there since day one.

'Today is actually a very special day for us. Its our fifty-second wedding anniversary.'

Margaret stopped fidgeting and looked up.

'This was the day she took a chance on a broke, balding fellow by saying, "I Do"', he said, with a wink in her direction.

'It is?' Margaret asked.

'Yes, sweetheart, it is.'

'Congratulations you two! Cook has made a lovely Victoria sponge today, and I'll make sure you both have some before you go. Are you having your usual today, Vegetable soup and chicken salad sandwiches?'

'Yes please', Jamie replied.

She nodded then went to walk away, but quickly turned back.

'I just remembered. We ran out of vegetable soup. Would tomato be okay?'

Jamie looked at his wife, now scrubbing away at the mark on the table with a napkin.

'Margaret?'

'Hmmm' she said, again focused on the table.

'They're out of vegetable soup. Do you want tomato? Or just a sandwich?' She looked confused, so he pointed to the menu and showed her a few other things he thought she would enjoy, but she was having a hard time focusing.

Suddenly, Margaret began to cry.

'I want to go home. Please can we go home' she begged.

'Sweetheart, Mary has already brought our drinks. Don't you think we should stay a wee bit longer. I know you like vegetable soup, but the tomato is just as delicious, it's all home made.'

That only made her cry harder. Mary apologised on behalf of the café, for them running out of soup. Other customers glanced in their direction, wondering what all the commotion was about.

He sighed, then took out his wallet and left a note on the table. 'I'm sorry, Mary. We'll catch you again next week.'

Mary gave him an understanding look, and told him that she would bring two takeaway cups of tea and two slices of cake out to their car. He thanked her as he helped Margaret out of her seat. He always tried to make her day as hiccup free as possible, but sometimes there just wasn't any vegetable soup.

Margaret stopped crying on the way home, but appeared anxious, and kept asking him what day it was. He hesitated to say the actual date, thinking that she was already upset enough. She just didn't seem to realise it was their anniversary. But with her dementia, he was worried she might become even more distressed if she realised the date.

'It's Wednesday', he replied.

She furrowed her brow, a telltale sign that she was struggling to grasp some distant memory or word.

When she asked what day it was for the third time, during their short journey home, he gave in.

'Its Wednesday the 24th of August.'

'That's the day we got married', she suddenly said, as if he had forgotten.

'Yes it is', he said with a smile, as he pulled into their driveway.

He helped Margaret into the house, and left her sitting on the couch, watching her favourite daytime quiz show.

'I'll be back soon, and we'll watch the TV together', he said.

Once in the kitchen he looked at all the cupboards. They were labelled – Bowls/Plates; Mugs/Glasses; Cereal, etc. until he came to the one labelled soup. He had marked them all to help her stay as independent as possible, as she had loved to cook. In the past few months, however, she had seemed to lose all interest and he had taken over all of the cooking. Jamie was relieved when he found a can of vegetable soup at the back of the cupboard.

Conscious of his stiff arthritic hands, he carefully lowered two bowls and filled them with soup before putting Margaret's bowl in the microwave. As he stood there watching the timer count down, the sound of their piano floated into the kitchen.

Margaret had been a music teacher, so they had always had a piano in the living room. She hadn't played much lately, though. He suspected it was because she now had difficulty reading the sheet music.

Walking back into the living room, he found Margaret bent over the piano playing Beethoven's Moonlight Sonata from muscle memory. He was amazed at how her fingers, still so capable and sure, glided over the keys. An image of her, coming down the aisle towards him, in a stunning white dress, came into his head. Those same lovely hands, holding a bouquet of yellow carnations that he had gathered that morning from his garden. It had been a simple wedding, but that is what they had both wanted.

He waited until she had finished playing, before sitting beside her on the piano stool. Bringing the back of her hand to his lips, he planted a kiss there, as she beamed the same beautiful smile she'd had on their wedding day.

'My favourite song', he whispered, choking up.

She squeezed his hand gently. 'That is why I played it for you.'

Now it was his turn to cry.

'I love you Jamie', she said.

'I can see that', he nodded.

'I love you too, my darling. Now how would you like to share some vegetable soup with me?'

Her face fell a little.

'I was hoping for tomato soup, but I suppose that will do!'

HOW DID THAT HAPPEN?

Mary

It occurred to Mark that he must have walked past that shop thousands of times over the course of the last twenty or so years going to and from his office but paid no attention to it. But today it was different, on his way home he felt compelled to stop and peer through the dusty glass. Something had caught his attention but why today he couldn't say. A shaft of autumnal sunlight fell on a dusty black box, almost as if it were under a spotlight, dust motes lazily danced in the pale light spiralling down to settle on the box.

To call the shop an antique shop was to give it far too grand a title, it was first and foremost a junk shop – but what treasures did it contain?

Mark pushed open the door and stepped inside. His first reaction was that he had entered a time warp where nothing had changed in the last fifty or more years. He heard a bell ring somewhere in the depths of the gloomy rooms. Looking around the shop there didn't appear to be any kind of order to the contents, a mishmash of items not displayed, just giving the impression of being tossed into the window, onto the shelves, tables and floor to rest where they fell.

Mark made his way with care to the window for a closer look at the black box. It appeared, at first glance, to be made of some sort of black metal and had once been richly decorated the gilding having been worn away over time. It was old but something about the small box with its worn decoration appealed to him.

Mark knew his wife and daughter were exasperated over his hoarding capabilities, he preferred the term collecting, remembering only too well the upset caused by their last decluttering done without asking him. He could see in his mind's eye the pitying look his daughter had perfected whenever he came home with his latest curio.

He wondered if there was anyone on the premises and as he turned to leave a tiny woman appeared from the gloom. She had the appearance of a small bird with bright black button eyes that danced with merriment. She was dressed from head to toe in brown, a long brown dress with an old fashioned brown shawl over her shoulders. Mark immediately thought of the little brown wren he had seen in his garden, even more so when she walked towards him, her movements quick and bobbing. She smiled up at him, her eyes almost disappearing into the criss-cross of wrinkles that covered her face. When she spoke, enquiring how she may help, her voice was a soft almost inaudible whisper.

Mark explained his interest in the box to which the birdlike woman, whom Mark had named Jenny, replied that it had been there almost as long as she had but didn't offer anything by way of explanation as to how long that was.

Jenny made her way delicately to the window to remove the box disturbing the dust as she did so, she handed the box to Mark. Close up now he could see how very worn the box was, much loved he thought. It was not large, about six inches long by four wide and two deep. The gilding was so worn that he couldn't really make it out but there appeared to be several figures but it was impossible to see what they were. Mark turned the box over in his hands assuming it was empty, there was no weight to it, nothing moved inside and when he tried to open it the catch appeared to be jammed.

Mark didn't understand why the box held such a fascination for him, it wasn't rational but he knew he just had to have it regardless of the family's feelings about him and his collecting.

A few minutes later Mark was leaving the shop with the box tucked protectively under his left arm and a look of anticipation on his face as he walked to the station and the train home. Once on the train he stowed the box carefully in his briefcase away from his wife's looks of exasperation.

Later that same evening found Mark in his garage trying to open the box. After several unsuccessful attempts he managed to prise the lid open using the thin blade of a Stanley knife. Mark wasn't expecting to find anything inside so he was surprised to find the box was not empty but was stuffed with a cream coloured muslin-like fabric which was discoloured along the folds. He took the cloth out and shook it and from the folds a ring fell onto his work bench. Mark stared at the ring before he picked it up with trembling hands to look at it more closely. It was a beautiful oval cut sapphire of the deepest blue surrounded by a halo of brilliant cut diamonds which sparkled in the light.

He stared at the ring for what seemed like an age, he knew this ring having seen it worn by his grandmother. Granny died some years ago and the ring disappeared shortly after amidst much speculation as to its whereabouts, but the general consensus was that it had been removed by a family member.

So what was granny's ring doing in an old worn black box in a messy junk shop?

FORBIDDEN FRUIT – Take 2

Lynda A

Whenever her mind turned to thoughts of him, she pictured olives. Not just any olives, but the lush, juicy, rich brown olives languishing in their oil that the Turkish women sold at the local street market.

These succulent olives reminded her of his eyes, soft and brown as they gazed at her, eyes full of tenderness; his eyes hot with desire for her when they lay together side by side on the crumpled bed in her hotel room. Eyes that promised her everything – love, lust and passion.

Those same olives reminded her of the smooth brown skin that covered his perfect muscular body, the body she loved to stroke as he gently caressed her on the crumpled bed in her hotel room.

When she saw leeks, carrots, courgettes, she thought of him. She saw again, in her mind's eye, the outline of a seemingly continual erection straining against the tight trousers that were his uniform. She considered the promise that outline held after the arid sex life that had been her marriage.

Peaches reminded him of her. The tones of colour that were reflected in her skin; both had that light covering of down, both offering the anticipation of sweet juicy flesh within; their perfume an aphrodisiac to the senses – ripe and succulent.

They met in Turkey.

She was an American woman, nearing menopause, travelling to escape the memories of an ignominious divorce, hoping to regain her self-confidence; enjoying the irresponsibility of her mid-life crisis – at last becoming a person in her own right, someone who could make her own decisions.

He was a tourist guide, young, athletic and good looking, constantly admired – sometimes from afar (a long lingering look when his attention was elsewhere), occasionally more assertively (when one of his flock would monopolise his time and attention, stick by his side, touch him to emphasise in conversation). She had been one of the former, and in her he had sensed a desperation that had attracted him. That desperation could lead to the one thing he desired most in the world, a US visa, a way out of the not-much-hope future that was his.

After eighteen months of phone calls, letters, and visits to Turkey, they were finally married – a traditional wedding in his village. Then came the interminable paperwork required for the much sought-after visa. They were married, she longed for the consummation of their wedding vows, but this was denied to them until they could live as one. He anticipated their life together in that far-off land of opportunity that was America.

At last, three years after their original meeting, visa in passport, he landed at JFK and ran straight into her arms.

Now she can no longer contemplate those olives that she had once gazed at so longingly. A myopic blue gaze replaced the hot, passionate brown eyes when he removed his tinted contact lenses. The skin that she had loved to stroke had become pale and flaccid in the New York climate.

Now, when she notices okra she thinks of him. That seemingly continual erection had been a fake, good for attracting the women and getting larger tips. Leeks, carrots and courgettes had been eliminated from her diet, preferring not to be reminded of her disappointment.

For him too, the juicy anticipation of peaches had dried; with the disappointment of his reality, she no longer turned to him in their marital bed. The promise that had been his vision of life in the US had also turned stale. The only work he could find had been manual labour in a fish factory, the odour of which lingered on his skin, reducing further his attractiveness to his wife.

And so they exist side by side, in a marriage devoid of love, communication or mutual interests. He dreams of his homeland, of the sun on his skin, of the blue Mediterranean and the adoring women tourists. She dreams of the life she had envisaged for herself after the death of her first marriage, those new stirrings of optimism.

But surely everyone knows that peaches and olives should not be stored together, that they will become putrid.

THE LONELY STRANGER

Bryony

Last night I saw him again – so he has not given up his vigil. As it was a bit chilly he was stood in the doorway of the empty shop opposite. When I look out of my bedroom window I have sometimes noticed him sitting on the corner outside the kebab shop. On other occasions I have seen him standing by the bus stop. I have never seen him arrive so I do not know from which direction he comes but as regular as clockwork every evening around 8.30 he appears. I do not know how long he waits but he is usually still there when I go to bed. However on the odd occasion when I have looked out in the middle of the night after a bathroom visit he has not been there. But by 8.30 I know that he will be there somewhere. I had begun to get obsessed with his presence and for a week I had forced myself not to look out for him but I could not resist looking again last night. I have only lived in this house for a couple of months so I wonder for how long he has been coming.

He looks quite lean and has unruly slightly wavy hair that glints brown and gold in the street lights. He has dark eyes that are alert to everything that passes. What or who is he waiting or looking for? I am resolved to investigate so I decide that the next night I will go for a walk around the time he arrives as the nights are getting lighter now. I do not feel bothered by his presence but I am curious about his apparently fruitless waiting.

As I put on my coat the next evening I feel a sense of purpose in what I am doing. I look out of the window – and yes he is there in the shop doorway. I walk slowly past him and his eyes follow me. I cannot see a collar but it might be hidden deep in his neck fur. As I return to walk back past him I say,

'Hello boy – what are you doing here?'

Of course he does not reply but his tail wags energetically. In my pocket I have a chewy stick which I slowly take out and I am pleased that he eagerly but gently takes it from me. I do not presume more as it is our first meeting but I resolve to bring another tasty treat tomorrow. As I cross the road I feel him watching me and when I turn he looks at me quizzically.

I repeat the procedure for the next few nights and tonight he has decided to wait by my gate. I dare to hold out my hand for him to sniff and he licks it. I am aware of the man who lives next door out in his front garden and as he leans over his wall to talk to me the dog makes a low growl.

'He doesn't like me because I used to try and chase him away for his own good', said the man.

'Why would you do that – he means no harm?' I said rather sharply.

'I hoped he would get the message and realise that his family no longer live in your place. He used to bark outside the door for hours on end which was driving the neighbours mad and some of them threatened to call the dog warden. He stopped coming for a while but I have noticed that since you moved in he has returned again. Perhaps it is seeing lights on and movement in the house again that has made him come back?'

'How sad! Why didn't his owners take him with them when they left?'

'That's a sorry tale', he sighed, 'There was a couple with a little girl who lived there with the dog which they got for the child one Christmas. They were a lovely family – very close – but one day I saw an ambulance outside and the little girl was taken to hospital. She never returned and the neighbours the other side of you said that she had leukaemia and died. After that the woman left and it was just the man and the dog, but he turned to drink and drugs and ended up inside and the dog was just abandoned. Then the house was empty for around a year until it was bought by a builder at auction and renovated before you moved in.'

'Poor dog – what a shame. Do you know who owns him now?'

'Nobody owns him. He has become a street dog and scavenges where he can. They feed him over the road at the kebab shop when they have leftovers and I have heard that he is good at toppling over the bins to see what he can find. People say that he lives in a shed at the back of the derelict house in the next street – but I really don't know. By the way his name is Baxter – or that's what the little girl used to call him.'

Over the weeks I continued to feed Baxter at the usual time buying him proper dog food and I always left him a bowl of water in the front garden for during the day in case he passed by. One day he was there when I came home from work which was unusual but then I noticed that he had brought a friend with him – a very pregnant bitch that looked like a cross between a poodle and a spaniel.

'Is this your doing?' Baxter wagged his tail proudly. 'So now I have the two of you to feed do I?' So every evening I catered for both of them.

A couple of weeks later Baxter came on his own again but he was very agitated and refused to eat. He kept walking away and stopping then barking and coming back. It seemed as if he wanted me to follow him so I grabbed a jacket, phone and my keys and we set off. As the man next door had said Baxter led me to an empty house in the next street and he ducked in under the back gate to the garden. I was not keen to follow him as it was trespassing but he started barking again.

'Alright boy – I will see if I can climb over the gate.'

I managed to get over without being seen and followed him to the end of the garden where there was an old shed and inside was the female dog and a puppy. But it was obvious that things were not right as the mother was not moving and she felt cold to the touch although her tail gave a slight wag when I approached.

I had no choice but to call the RSPCA who told me that they would try to save the puppy as they had a dog at their centre who had just given birth so she might accept the pup. But that the mother looked beyond help and would probably have to be euthanised. They tried to catch Baxter but to no avail. I told the inspector about his sad background and they said that they would try to rehome him and to ring them if he reappeared at my place.

I did not see Baxter again for a week and I began to worry that he no longer trusted me. Then one stormy evening when I got home he was outside my door again. He looked so forlorn and unhappy that there was no way that I was going to get him picked up and taken away by the RSPCA before at least giving him a good meal. As I opened my front door to find him some food unusually he walked ahead of me into the hall and stood there as if asking permission to come in.

'OK – you can eat inside today if you want as it is so wet.'

Baxter walked into the kitchen all the time looking around him curiously.

'I guess it has changed a lot since you were last here', I said.

I opened a can and he gobbled it down quickly as he was obviously very hungry so I gave him some biscuits as well. He then sauntered towards the living room and inspected it while I got on with preparing my dinner. After a while he returned and stood by the back door asking to go out so I left the door ajar and after he had relieved himself he came and lay down beside me while I was cooking. It was such a wet and windy night that I decided to let him stay with me then call the RSPCA in the morning. I put an old blanket on the floor and he soon settled and went to sleep.

I let him out again before I went up to bed and in the morning he was where I had left him looking quite at home. So could I now make that phone call?

'I hadn't planned to have a dog you know. So if I decided to let you live here you would have to have a bath as you are a bit smelly to put it mildly and a vet check-up in case you have worms or the like – so what do you think?'

It was almost as if he understood me as he got up from the blanket and sat down before me presenting his paw to seal the deal.

So now after a visit to the dog groomer for a bath and trim which he tolerated without complaint, and a visit to the vet which was equally without protest even following injections and worming pills – he is a new man!

And as I look across to him stretched out on the rug beside me fast asleep I am glad that he came my way as we have got into a routine and have both gained the companionship and love that we needed in our lives.

THE CHRISTMAS PRESENT

Linda H

Catherine Thompson looked out of her farmhouse window at the view, although it was lovely, there was no other house in sight. This suited Catherine as she had never been a woman to crave company. She liked sewing and was passionately fond of reading. The whole world had opened up to her when she learnt to read as a lonely child living on the farm. She was not fond of talking, and preferred the peace and quiet of farm life.

Probably she would have been happier at the farm alone. Before her marriage she had looked forward to the long evenings with her sewing and reading. She was kept busy enough during the day with farm work and housework and had always looked forward to quiet peaceful evenings. But lately, after ten years of married life, she had given up all hope of them. Peace was far from her life these days. It was driven away by John Thompson's loud voice; raised always in orders or complaints; or in the stumbling, incoherent reading aloud of his newspaper.

Catherine was a silent woman herself and a lover of silence. But John liked to hear the sound of his own voice; he liked to shout at her; to call for her from one room to another; above all he liked to hear his voice reading the paper out loud to her in the evenings. She dreaded that most of all. It jarred on her nerves until she felt she must scream aloud. His voice going on and on. His, 'Catherine!' summoning her from her housework to wherever he happened to be. His cries of, 'Get my slippers', or 'Bring me my newspaper', exasperated her almost to the point of rebellion.

'Get your own slippers', had trembled on her lips, but had never passed them, for she could not bear anger. Loud noise of any kind appalled her. She had put up with it for ten years, so surely she could go on with it. But something had to happen. He was getting louder.

It was Christmas next week and as usual, they would spend Christmas Day with her aunt and uncle. She always looked forward to that. John always grumbled about the invitation at first, as her aunt was as deaf as a post, but really he liked to go. He liked going down into town for the day and going to the pub with her uncle to hear all the gossip. The Wyllie deafness was proverbial. Catherine's great-grandmother had gone deaf at the age of thirty-five; her daughter (Catherine's grandmother) had inherited the affliction, and then her eldest daughter, Catherine's aunt Mary, had gone deaf at exactly the same age.

Soon it was Christmas Eve. They travelled down to her aunt and uncle's house early as the snow was starting to fall. The deaf old woman sat in her chair knitting. Upon her face there was the curious sardonic smile that was her habitual expression. Uncle Jim shouted to let her know that they had arrived. 'Mary', he said. She never stirred. 'Mary', he said a bit louder. Still there was no response upon the enigmatic old face. 'Mary!' He shouted really loudly this time. She turned slightly towards the voice, and smiled when she realised they had come early.

John nodded towards her, 'Is she getting worse?' Jim shrugged his shoulders, 'Aye, she's as bad as her mother was, and her grandmother. It takes so long to tell her to do something that I just end up doing it myself. And deaf folks get a bit stupid too. So it's best just to leave her alone'.

He looked out the window. 'The snow's stopped. Do you fancy a few beers at the pub, John?'

After they left, Catherine sat down and took a book out of her bag as she knew she wouldn't be able to have a conversation with her aunt.

'Catherine?' She started as her aunt was leaning forward and looking at her intently. 'Catherine, a happy Christmas to you.'

Catherine answered in her normal tone, forgetting to raise her voice, 'The same to you Aunty'.

'Thank you.'

Catherine gasped. 'Aunty. Can you hear me?'

The old woman laughed. 'Yes, I can hear you. I've always heard you'.

'So you're cured, Aunty.'

'Yes I can hear, but there was never anything to be cured.'

'You what?'

'I was never deaf Catherine, nor never will be, please God. I've taken you all in.'

Catherine stood up in bewilderment. 'You've never been deaf?'

The old woman laughed again. 'No, nor my mother, nor her mother neither'.

'I don't know what you mean' said Catherine. 'Have you been pretending?'

'I'll make you a Christmas present of the secret my dear. My mother made me a Christmas present of it when I was your age, and her mother made her one. I haven't got a daughter of my own to give it to. So I give it to you. It can come on sudden like, if you want it, and then you can just hear what you choose or not hear what you choose. Do you see? You don't have to fetch and carry for them; answer their daft questions and run their errands like a dog. I've watched you my lass and you don't get much peace do you?'

Catherine was trembling. 'Oh I don't know aunty. I don't think I could do it.'

'It's up to you', said her aunt. 'Take it as a present anyways – the Wyllie deafness as a Christmas present', she chuckled. 'Use it or not, as you like. You'll find it amusing anyway.'

They heard the men returning, and again onto that old face came the curious smile.

'We didn't stay long. It's snowing again', Uncle James said as they both came in, shattering the peace, talking loudly to each other. Aunt Mary began to set the table and moved around without looking up. 'Any sign of the deafness in her?' Uncle James whispered to John, looking towards Catherine. 'It came on Mary, just about the same age.'

Then he said very loudly, 'Catherine, Catherine?'

Her husband John also shouted to her. 'Answer your uncle, woman.'

A faint pink colour came into her cheeks but she did not show, by look or movement that she had heard. Uncle James looked at her husband and shook his head.

'I think its started, son', he said quietly.

Aunt Mary just stood still for a moment with a cup in each hand and smiled her slow subtle smile.

MEMORIES

Mary

Dawn was breaking, the sun not yet risen but the skyline turning various shades of gold, pink, crimson and lilac to herald in another beautiful day. The waves lapped lazily against the wall of the promenade with its wrought iron railings and seats. The fronds of the palm trees just swaying in the gentle warm breeze.

An elderly man was sitting watching the sunrise, an equally elderly black, tan and white rough coated terrier-type dog sitting quietly at his feet. Every sunrise would see the two of them, Pascal and his little dog, on the same seat taking in the gentle warmth before the heat of the day drove them to seek shelter.

He cut a rather forlorn figure in his worn shirt and trousers, a battered hat, no longer white, covered lank hair the ends of which curled over the collar of his shirt like something live. The years had not been kind leaving him a face pitted with acne scars, hair protruding from his nose and ears, most of his teeth had been lost over the years due to fights and neglect. And he dribbled.

As a young man he had been fairly good looking, the acne scars adding a bad boy image. A sailor with a girl in every port as the saying goes but in this instance it was true and he was proud of his reputation.

His life on merchant ships took him all over the world from the icy seas of the north to the warmth of the Caribbean and Mediterranean.

Nice on the French Riviera was one of his regular ports of call, not the glamorous place which attracted the rich and famous but the port area, dirty, scruffy and drab. His favourite haunt was a scruffy seamen's café in one of back streets of the port, here he met up with shipmates from previous voyages and they put the world to rights and drank copious amounts of alcohol, any alcohol.

He had a girl in Nice but she didn't mean a lot to him. He certainly wasn't faithful to her and he was aware she wasn't faithful to him, it was just a convenience.

On one visit to the port Pascal and several of his mates from the ship decided to have a look at the other side of Nice, an area they rarely went. They wandered along the wide streets lined with palm trees, exclusive boutiques and restaurants. On turning a corner they found themselves outside an art gallery exhibiting works by the artist Salvador Dali. Pascal said he thought it would be a good idea to visit but his mates were less than enthusiastic saying it was rubbish. Pascal noticed a small card on the door which told him that the exhibition would be opened that evening by an actress he had seen in a film not that long ago.

Pascal decided to go along to see her but he didn't really know why, he just knew he had to be there. His mates laughed and jeered at him as they were off to the bars in the port area for a good time.

Pascal made an effort, he washed and put on clean clothes and went on his way to the gallery. Did he look out of place? Yes. Did he care? No, he was on a mission. He was late so by the time he reached the gallery the opening had taken place, the actress long gone. Of course Pascal didn't know this. The function was in full swing with people coming and going.

The Dali exhibition was by invitation only so how was he to get in? Security was in place but as the doors opened to allow guests to leave and security was temporarily distracted Pascal managed to sneak inside.

Then he saw her, tall and slender, dark hair framing an oval face. But it was her eyes, mesmerising blue. He had no idea who she was but he just had to be near her. As she passed him their eyes met, he was transfixed by her beauty. He watched as she left the building, determined to find out who she was and where she was going, he followed her out and saw her get into a large silver car which sped away into the night.

There was nothing else to do but go back to the ship where his mates later tried unsuccessfully to find out whether he had managed to get into the gallery.

The following day Pascal returned to the area of the gallery and asked questions at the back door of nearby restaurants. He learned that she was the youngest daughter of a Russian oligarch who had recently bought a property in the area.

A long exhausting walk in the heat brought him to a large gated mansion on a hill overlooking the ocean. He tried to gain access to the grounds but was thwarted at every turn by the high walls and gates which he just could not find a way over.

It was just a dream anyway. So after a short rest in the shade of a nearby hedge Pascal started out on the long hot walk back to the ship. He hadn't gone far when he heard the throaty purr of an expensive sports car engine. The car drew up beside him, it was her, those beautiful eyes hidden behind a pair of large designer sunglasses. She asked could she give him a lift anywhere. Of course he jumped at the chance of spending some time with her. They were poles apart but once they started talking it was as if they had known each other for forever. He explained that he had to go away the next day but would be returning a month later. They made tentative arrangements to meet at a small café out of the city but Pascal didn't really think that she would remember.

A month later his ship returned to the port. Pascal had not forgotten her and the arrangement made. His shore leave started the following day and Pascal awoke with a feeling of nervous anxiety knotting his stomach – would she be there?

He left for the meeting place, the small café out of the city. Again it was a long hot walk but as he turned into the car park and saw her sports car there his heart sang. She ran out into his arms and he held her tightly. Suddenly he was aware of a large man behind her dragging her away screaming and another man coming towards him. Pascal reached into the belt of his jeans for the knife he always carried there, there was a flash of the blade as the knife arced through the air, the man approaching him screamed, the scream cut short as the knife found its mark. Pascal froze, he could not believe what he had done, he dropped the knife and backed away turning to run but his exit was blocked by several more burly minders. There was no escape.

Many years later after his release from prison Pascal would sit on the promenade watching the sunrise, an elderly man, with his dog, alone with his memories.

SKIN

Lynda A

At first Jude thought it was a snowflake as something fluttered to the ground, but on inspection the sky was blue and cloudless; similar odd flakes went unnoticed as her mind was still focused on the meeting she had recently addressed, which had proved immensely stressful.

Once home, as she was removing her coat, she noticed more flakes falling from her coat. She assumed she must have dandruff but was puzzled by the size of the flakes as she thought dandruff was quite fine. On looking in the mirror to check her head she noticed that her facial skin was looking extremely dry and very patchy; the makeup she had worn to give her talk was flaking off.

As she only wore makeup to hide behind on special occasions she supposed that she was allergic to that particular brand and threw the foundation away as soon as she had removed the concealing mask.

The following day, on awakening, she discovered rather a lot of dead skin flakes not just on her pillow but on the bottom sheet too, from the head of the bed to its base.

It was all rather bizarre.

Her doctor could shed no light on her problem and suggested they make an appointment with a skin specialist.

The dermatologist, who she was very lucky to see the following week due to a cancelled appointment, took scrapings of her skin from various parts of her face and body to be sent away for analysis. He thought that it could be an allergic reaction to something . . . makeup, soap powder, cleaning fluids being the usual candidates that she could eliminate from use until they received the results of the skin scrapings.

Nothing seemed to have any effect on her skin loss, if anything, it was getting worse by the day; it was also becoming painful. Jude was given a month off work owing to stress, so she was able stay at home and thus avoid wearing her usual business suits which would have irritated her raw, tender body.

When the skin analysis came back it shed not a glimmer of light on what was causing her skin loss; the dermatologist prescribed various creams and ointments, all of which she tried, none of which made a blind bit of difference. But she kept trying; she assumed that at some point it would all just go back to normal . . . after all, she was a young fit woman in the prime of life.

That notion got a nasty knock on the head when one morning, as Jude got out of bed, she noticed that she had left her right ear on the pillow.

It had just dropped off!

Luckily she was able to arrange an emergency home visit from her GP. He was almost as shocked by the sight of Jude's ear sitting on the pillow as she had been. He was also surprised at the amount of dead skin he could see decorating her bed especially, but basically her entire apartment was thus coated.

Jude noticed his eyes taking in her skin-laden flat and explained that it was yesterday's droppings . . . that she Hoovered her bed and floor every morning but had been shocked to immobility by the ear loss so hadn't yet Hoovered that day.

At least the loss of her ear could be covered by her hair . . . not that anyone else would see, she hadn't been outside for nearly a month, she had her vegetables doorstep-delivered every week along with milk and yoghurt, she didn't need anything else.

She was granted early retirement on health grounds following a strong letter from her doctor to her company who still thought the stress of her job had caused her problems. She was allotted a part-time carer to visit her on a daily basis and help with the things she found she was incapable of doing.

Before long she had lost all her hair and nails (she had tried super glue to stick the nails back onto her fingers, but they just took the skin off with them), a couple of toes and a little finger. Her actual skin coverage was depleting on an hourly basis revealing muscle, tendon and ligament in their raw form.

As nobody seemed to know the base cause of the demise of her skin and body parts, Jude decided to work on logic to devise a treatment for herself. She put in an order for a vast quantity of olive oil to be delivered to her house, which she then instructed the carer to pour into the bath; at the same time she ordered miles of clingfilm. Every morning she would climb into the bath and submerge herself in the oil (don't worry, she had a non-slip mat on the base of her bath); on exiting the carer would wrap her oil-soaked body and head in a clingfilm coating, leaving her face uncovered but with an oily coating; disposable gloves held her hands together and allowed her the freedom to carry out some actions like picking up her coffee.

Jude came to the realisation that her body was never really going to heal from whatever was ailing it; she had actually become fascinated by watching her muscles working beneath their clingfilm wrap, seeing the difference between the ligaments and tendons which were particularly evident in her hands each time she used them. Of course she was lonely . . . most, in fact all, of her 'friends' had been her work colleagues, none of whom contacted her after she was given early retirement; after all, they were all stressed too and they didn't really believe she'd been ill enough to need to retire.

She relied heavily on her carer for physical help, especially with the morning shrouding; lately she had realised she needed more help with food preparation, housework etc. which she had found increasingly difficult. Her doctor suggested that she apply for ESA, she managed to fill out the long, in-depth application form with help from her carer (holding a pen and writing with oil covered, disposable glove protected, hands is not the easiest thing in the world). Despite the fact that she had no skin, hair or nails she was expected to attend an appointment at the local centre so they could assess her capability to work and her eligibility to receive ESA.

How could she possibly go out, to an office, and undergo such as assessment . . . she knew that she looked grotesque.

She now Googled the question, 'How long can a person exist without skin?'

The response was a shock . . . no longer than a day because of the probability of infection! Well, that was wrong; she had now lived/existed for three months with no skin, apart from her clingfilm excuse for a skin . . . but now she realised that she could not go out in public and risk getting infected. So she had to pass on ESA and look for an alternative source of income.

She decided to sell her story to any women's magazine or newspaper that was interested . . . photographs would have to be taken through the window to avoid infection and she could be interviewed over the phone. As you can imagine a lot of the media she contacted were interested, this was an unknown and gruesome illness and would sell even more magazines than stories like, 'My mother had sex with a bear which is why I am so hirsute', and, 'My own son tried to kill me when he was four years old'. Soon the hideous photos of her body were gracing magazines on all major supermarket shelves . . . luckily for her they had paid her enough for the privilege that she had enough to cover her extra living costs for the next six months and in all truth, how likely was it that she would last any longer than that?

You can also find her posthumously in the *Guinness Book of Records* . . . she had lived for eight months with no skin . . . I should mention that she was the only person for whom there was any evidence of this condition, so there was no competition.

On her death her body was bought by Damien Hirst and placed into a glass container filled with a formaldehyde solution . . . it was to be his next entry for the Turner Prize . . . we'll have to see how that goes.

HOME

Bryony

The room was very basic – just a narrow metal bed with a thin striped mattress, a small white chipboard chest of drawers, a hard plastic table and chair, and a couple of hooks on the wall – but to Lisa it was a palace.

She had spent the last six months living rough on the streets, and had endured hunger, cold, thirst, abuse and much more. Sometimes – when it came to the choice between defying the elements and sharing a stranger's bed – the instinct for survival had kicked in. But this did not always leave her in a good place in the morning, although most of the time she had learned to switch off her emotions. Her mother had left her and her brother with Social Services when she was only five. After many foster parents and her last two years in care she had been sent out into society to fend for herself. She had been found accommodation in a shared house but she soon fell behind with the rent, and was evicted because she had never been taught how to manage her money. So at the age of seventeen she found herself with a few meagre possessions and nowhere to go. After a particularly cold night she had been found unconscious in a doorway suffering from exposure and malnutrition. Lisa had been admitted to hospital where she stayed for over a week. Social Services then placed her in temporary accommodation, and eventually she was found a room at this small hostel where she could be supported and helped.

Social Services had given her some blankets, sheets and a pillow – also trainers, jeans, jumpers and tops, and socks and underwear. She made up her bed and carefully folded away her clothing in the drawers. She had been given some money to buy food and toiletries until her benefit was sorted out – so she sat at the table and thought about what she needed to buy. She had been told that she would be allocated a cupboard in which to store her food in the communal kitchen area, and that she would be given set times to use the cooking facilities when she would be able to use the utensils, pans and crockery. Lisa made her way downstairs to find out about the kitchen regime. She could smell food cooking and followed her nose. The kitchen area was old fashioned but clean. There were three large cookers, two sinks, various cupboards and a large fridge and freezer. In an annexe she could see a row of cupboards with names on – many of which were decorated with stickers and pictures. There were three girls of Lisa's age being given a lesson in food preparation by a middle-aged woman with a kind face and a raucous laugh. She was warmly welcomed and introduced, and invited to have a cup of tea and a slice of a freshly baked sponge cake while the procedures relating to the kitchen were explained to her. Lisa was then helped to make up a basic food list to provision her cupboard, and she then set off to the local supermarket.

After purchasing most of the items on her list she decided to wander a bit further to get familiar with the area and came across some houses that were being renovated. Outside was a skip and she noticed that on the top of the old timber and rubble a cardboard box was resting. She could not resist looking into it – but just as she did so one of the workmen appeared and asked what she thought she was doing. She must have looked frightened as his gaze softened and he told her that she was welcome to help herself if anything in the box was of use to her. There were a lot of cheap ornaments, some paperbacks, a decorated candle, a piece of white coral and a strangely shaped brown pottery object. As she did not want to appear greedy Lisa checked with the workman that it was alright to take the candle and a couple of paperbacks. But he insisted that she also take the coral and the strange pottery object.

'I'll take the rest of the books back for the wife – and probably chuck the other stuff', he told her.

Back in her room Lisa placed the coral and the candle on her chest of drawers and the brown pottery object (which someone downstairs had told her was a tagine – something to do with foreign cooking) on the table. She thought that perhaps it would look nice with a flower in it – it was nearly spring so there would be plenty of wildflowers down by the canal. She looked around her room which she had now made look like home, and for the first time in months she felt safe, secure and happy. Then she curled up on the bed with one of the paperbacks – but soon fell peacefully and deeply asleep for the first time in months.

THE STORY COLLECTOR

Linda H

Everyone has a story to tell. That is, everyone apart from me. So, what then, I became a collector of other people's stories.

I can't recall what started my collection. Maybe it was other lives glimpsed as I rode on the bus to work. I have worked as a cleaner for several years now. Or something in a fragment of conversation overheard, as I cleaned a sink or a toilet. Before long, as I dusted a sitting room or defrosted a fridge, I noticed that people also liked to tell me their stories.

As I listen to their stories, the small nod that I give acknowledges what I know to be true, that I am a simple homely bowl into which they can pour their confidences.

Often the stories are unexpected; at times they are funny and engaging; sometimes they are steeped in regret. I think people talk to me because I believe in their stories. At home at night I think about all the stories and overheard conversations. My life has always been uneventful and it's the prospect of glimpses of other people's eventful lives that helps get me out of bed and strengthens me for the day ahead.

I've discovered that a good cleaner can pretty much dictate their days and hours, and more importantly, the order in which I do cleaning on any particular day. Everyone knows that reliable cleaners are hard to come by and my employers have discovered that I am very good. I even overheard one of my employers saying that I was 'exceptional', when she had a friend in for coffee. I know I'm not an exceptional woman, but am I a good cleaner? Yes, I think I am. I have certainly had enough practice.

I just hope this isn't going to be the sum story of my life. I don't want my epitaph to be, 'She cleaned well'.

On Monday morning as I get off the bus at Kingsbridge Avenue, I look across the road to a long leafy avenue of detached houses. I imagine there are many stories hidden behind all those windows. My first house to clean is the rambling Edwardian house on the corner. Geordie has lived here for over forty years. Originally he took a room as lodger. Then eventually, when he married, he ended up buying the house from his landlady, Over the years they had many tenants. So, along with the fact that he was also a famous tenor, meant that he had many tales to tell. My time cleaning for him is more fun than work. He will often sing me one of his favourite arias as I clean his oven.

Today, he has a story about a posh twat mouthing off on the tube, on his recent trip to London. He even did a pretty good imitation of the 'posh tosser', making me grin. I had been right; Geordie was the place to start my day, my week.

After a coffee with Geordie, I go on to my next client. Mrs Stride lives a few minutes walk from Kingsbridge Avenue, but in a very modest bungalow. She also keeps me amused with her stories of her friend, Enid. Enid is very much into one-upmanship. If Mrs Stride has a few days break at the seaside, then Enid has a holiday booked to the Bahamas. When I know that she is due to visit, I do some baking for Mrs Stride, but Enid always comments on the lovely patisserie, near her house!

Before I go home, I pop into the library to change my book. As I walk up the steps. I overhear yet another conversation. A young man coming down the steps is talking earnestly to a young woman and I overhear a snippet.

'Of course, I normally enter my peas into the Garden Show, but this year I have been growing turnips and decided to enter them too. I was so surprised when I won first prize for the biggest turnip. And, of course, the flowers were such a shock.'

I will never know why the flowers were such a shock, as the doors into the library closed behind me.

Soon I am back on the bus, and on my way home.

I am tired and as I sit down, I empty my mind and prepare to idly tune in to the conversations around me. I don't consider it eavesdropping. I let the talk wash over me, but occasionally I catch at the thread of a story. My journey is only half an hour, but it occupies my time.

This afternoon I overhear snippets but no real stories.

'He was late yet again', says a lady behind me.

A young man two seats away, 'Have you heard of Banana Jack Daniels?'

His companion replied, 'That sounds gross'.

He came back with, 'It is. But I can't get enough of the stuff!'

As they stand up, two women sit down in their seats. They are talking away like old friends.

'I was walking through the theatre car park and there he was.'

'Who?'

'You know . . . that actor. He's in everything.'

'Hugh Bonneville?'

'No, not him. He was in *The Observer* last week. You must have seen the article.'

'Bill Nighy?'

'No, not him. He's black.'

'Bill Nighy's not black! Oh you mean the man in the car park. Was it Idris Elba?'

'No, he's older, he was in that film with . . .'

And at that point they are standing up to get off, and I never will know who the actor was. For a few minutes, I have my own guesses as I catch my reflection in the rain-streaked bus window, and I see the ghost of a smile on my face.

Soon, I am home and my husband Jack asks me about my day.

'It's good that you are so happy in your work.'

I've never actually said that, but I realise that I am.

The rest of the week passes quickly.

On Tuesday, I clean for Mr Mukerjee, who played for the under-21s Indian cricket team. He is full of stories of his days on the pitch.

Then on Wednesday, I get talking to a frail elderly lady in the launderette while I was washing a client's duvet. It turned out that she had been an air stewardess on the first commercial flight from London to New York. As she folded her satin-edged blankets, she said that her husband couldn't abide a duvet, and she told me of her years with Pan Am.

Before long, it is Friday afternoon and my last job of the week. Fiona has recently lost her husband. He was very young and his death was sudden. I let myself in, and there is a note on the hall table.

GONE TO THE DENTIST, MONEY ON THE KITCHEN TABLE.

I am relieved but then I feel guilty. Fiona loves to tell me stories of her late husband as I clean. But I know I can get the cleaning done much quicker without her around, and I also want to avoid the sadness that surrounds her.

I had laughter to start my week, and sadness to finish it.

Just a short bus journey home, but again, I overhear some funny conversations. Not that I can ever claim to develop a second sense of where a story will go. But that is the joy of being a story collector, you can find the unexpected just about anywhere. I don't think I will ever stop collecting other people's stories. Some day I will write them all down. Maybe even write a book. Perhaps I do have a story to tell.

MOVING ON

Mary

Elizabeth sighed. Not ready for the cocooned and insulated life of a retirement complex it had been a difficult long drawn-out process to reach the decision to downsize from the family home to a two-bedroomed bungalow with a small courtyard garden. The house was now on the market and her daughter Sue, son-in-law Simon and granddaughter Poppy were on their way over to help her to go through everything in the house she had shared with her husband Peter, and where they had brought up their two daughters Sue and Jackie. Each room, each item held memories, both happy and sad, of her life. The girls were gone, married with their own families, Jackie in Australia and Sue half a mile down the road. Peter gone too, dead these five years but always in her heart. Time to move on she decided reluctantly. She worried that the new owners wouldn't continue to care for the garden she had so lovingly tended and which looked so beautiful on this glorious summer's day, the roses at their best, jewel colours against the green of the trees and shrubs.

Elizabeth put the kettle on to make tea, she knew she was merely delaying the inevitable. The doorbell rang and the door opened to admit her visitors and willing helpers. After a cup of tea they decided to start in the loft and work their way down through the house room by room.

Simon went on ahead into the loft and began to bring down the many boxes stored there. Most of the content was junk, those things that might be useful one day but never were, and consigned to an ever-growing pile on the back lawn awaiting their final journey to the charity shop, the recycling centre or landfill. The few items whose fate Elizabeth wanted time to consider were in the dining room. Simon brought down a box which had been decorated with drawings of matchstick men, stylised flowers, rudimentary stars and a whole host of strange symbols, all faded now to a dull brown.

Poppy's eyes lit up, at last she thought, something interesting. She loved her grandma dearly but it certainly wasn't her idea of a fun-filled day going through boxes and boxes of old tat and at this rate it would take months to clear the house.

Elizabeth's eyes clouded as she caught sight of the box, she knew immediately what it contained although she hadn't thought of it or opened it for many, many years. This box contained all sorts of treasures from her life before marriage and family, wonderful memories of carefree days both with Peter, the love of her life, friends and relationships before she met him. She didn't want to open this box as there would be no argument, it was going to her new home.

Poppy pounced on the box with glee, she opened it carefully to reveal a sea of discoloured tissue paper, and there was no way of knowing what colour it had once been. She took out an odd-shaped item and carefully removed the tissue to reveal a small earthenware pot with a round base and almost triangular shaped lid, she knew it was a tagine.

Elizabeth was immediately transported back to North Africa and a backpacking trip taken with Peter in the early days of their relationship and long before they were married. It was the only time in their lives together that she had been unfaithful to him or even thought of doing so, the memory triggering guilt even now.

Ali was a beautiful man with deep dark eyes, she felt she would drown when he looked at her. His dark wavy hair and unusual pale coffee-coloured skin set him apart. It was never going to be anything other than a holiday romance as they were poles apart, different cultures, different religions and besides she was already beginning to think of a life with Peter. She often hoped that life had been kind to Ali, whether he has married and had a family. She hoped fervently that he had not been hurt during any of the many conflicts that had blighted the region in recent years.

Several more tissue-wrapped objects from her past were revealed including coloured stones, pebbles and sea glass picked up from far flung beaches and some nearer home. Each one evoking its own personal memory.

Poppy brought out a larger irregular shaped object which, when unwrapped, proved to be a piece of bleached coral which Elizabeth had found washed up on a beach in northern Queensland during a trip to visit her aunt in Cairns and managed to smuggle it back home for her keepsake box. Here it was all those years later. As she took the coral from Poppy she could feel the heat of the tropical sun on her skin and hear the sounds of the sea. Elizabeth marvelled at the scale of the memories each item was able to awaken after so many years.

The revelation of the items and their associated memories continued until there was just one item left, a round of tissue. Elizabeth couldn't quite remember what it was but as the tissue fell away and she caught sight of the cream-coloured candle with its faded flower and butterfly design. She laughed, remembering how she had covered it with black cloth not wishing to damage it, painted the word *bomb* in white and stuck indoor sparklers in the top, the holes were still there. It had been used as a prop in a comedy sketch performed with Peter when they were involved with the local amateur dramatics group. She remembered the ensuing panic and chaos when the sparklers were lit and began to fizz, the stage manager rushing onto the stage with a fire bucket and throwing water over the pretend 'bomb', Peter and herself. The audience were in hysterics believing it was part and parcel of the plot. Health and Safety wouldn't allow that to happen now. The candle didn't look any the worse for its impromptu soaking.

As the items were carefully repacked into the box that had been their home for so many years a feeling of peace come over Elizabeth, something she had not felt for some considerable time. Yes, these were material things each with its own special place in her past but the memories that they held were also in her heart and she would carry them wherever life took her.

THE MEAT PRODUCERS

Lynda A

The year is 2050.

Veganism and vegetarianism have taken the world by storm since 2020 resulting in thousands of acres being freed up to not only grow vegetables and vegetable proteins, which has almost eradicated world hunger, but also to reforest much of the world that had been deforested for cattle ranching, producing much cleaner air worldwide.

Monsanto and other producers of dangerous pesticides and Franken seeds went bankrupt in 2021 when their products were deemed hazardous to mankind; the entire agricultural system reverted to organic growing over a period of time depending on how degraded their soil had become due to growing GMO crops.

Things on earth had taken a giant leap into a completely sustainable direction.

But still there was a need, or more precisely a want, of meat among the leaders of the majority of countries worldwide.

After a disastrous Brexit the UK had found itself with a lot of imports but very few exports to balance the books. The government of the time decided that the UK should be the meat producers for the meat-lusting leaders. This would bring in a good revenue and provide work although, for some reason (known only by the government), the factory departments dealing with all aspects of the butchering of the meat would rely on robots; the work involving people was mainly in taking and packaging the already processed orders. The exception would be scientists working in a laboratory attempting to find variety in the meat products available . . . they would have to sign an Official Secrets Act form.

It was decided that the most productive source of meat would be human; everyone was healthy, thanks to eating organic foodstuff. This had the added bonus that people could work as they were being unknowingly raised for slaughter thus supplying the government with income tax. A law was passed requiring every couple to produce two children at least thus ensuring a continual supply of exportable goods.

Having tested human flesh themselves, the department of Environment, Food and Rural Affairs decided the flavour was veal, pork or goat so marketed the food as such; this was useful given the diverse nature of meat consumption in the various countries across the world. Leaders could order a selection based on similarities between the animal in question and human similarities; for example bacon is nigh on impossible to replicate from human flesh (at the moment . . . scientists are working very hard to create this alternative).

Available for order are the following at present:

'Veal' . . . Neck, Sirloin, Rump, Leg, Fillet, Stewing Steak, Mince and Sausages.

'Pork' . . . Shoulder, Leg, Mince and Sausages.

'Goat' . . . Shoulder, Neck, Loin and Sausages.

Of course the livestock has had no idea what is going on; in general life is good, everyone earns enough to live on in the few industries that survived Brexit, also in the service industry which had bloomed for its UK workers . . . pay was increased and hours shortened by necessity with the exit of workers from Europe following Brexit (employers soon found that when they improved working conditions that English people would work well).

Food is cheap as it is subsidised by the 'generous' government and gyms are free; after all a healthy, well-fed animal produces better and more flavourful meat

When the slaughterhouses get short of meat various sensors around the country select suitable donors . . . often from gymnasiums where meat for the Neck, Leg and Shoulder cuts are generally sourced (bodybuilding is encouraged); other cuts of the meat can be obtained randomly from any member of the population.

Explanations for the disappearance of these meat sources varies from stories of gymnasts going abroad for competitive reasons and being killed in a plane crash to entire families supposedly just moving to another part of the country . . . in fact mass 'movement' of whole groups of people has become so much the norm that nobody really pays attention any more, they just get on with their lives. There are government orphanages for children if both parents have been slaughtered, where the children can stay until they are old enough for either work or the slaughterhouse. The entire media is controlled by the government, so the livestock has no way of researching anything of importance.

Since the government introduced their meat exportation the FTSE has risen year on year. The 'remainers' and the 'leavers' are no longer at war with each other; after all . . . what's the point? Brexit has proved to be the boost to the economy that had been promised before the referendum despite a few hiccups.

THE OAK TREE

Bryony

Within the confines and shadow of the shelter that I have provided they sit close together whispering endearments to each other. He is just fourteen and she is a few months younger. They are not as worldly-wise and sexually experienced as some of the youngsters that have used the space lately so it is refreshing to celebrate their innocence and naivety. They have been meeting here for a few weeks now – snatched moments away from their peers – and today he gave her a silver necklace with a heart locket. They kissed for the first time – a gentle and sweet action barely making contact but nevertheless full of the joys of first love. The next time that they meet she will give him a lucky horseshoe key ring.

They will eventually marry but not until they have been separated for many years after he has returned from Afghanistan with PTSD and she has graduated from university to become a psychologist. She will keep the heart necklace in a trinket box in her bedroom and he will carry the lucky horse shoe to war with him. You may wonder how I know this so I can tell you that during my many years on this earth I have developed numerous talents and foretelling the future is one of them.

I am nearly nine-hundred years old although there are some (not many) who are even older than me. The shelter that I have created which has been used by many over the years was caused by a lightning strike which split me almost in two. However I was not to be defeated by such an act of nature and I grew back together leaving a large cavity at my base the size of a small room which has grown larger over the years. Some of my roots moved upwards to form seats of varying sizes which have been further moulded by those who have sought refuge within.

During World War Two I had the company of a village family on many occasions – parents with two children and their grandmother – who took shelter during air raids. I heard the father say that they would be safer within my trunk than in a man-made shelter as after all I had been around for years. They stored blankets, water, candles and tins of food within my trunk. They also made a shield with woven branches and tarpaulin to keep out the elements, protect from flying debris and provide some security as when it was in place it looked like thick undergrowth around my base. Their grandmother used to sing to the children to distract them from what was happening. She had a wonderfully sweet voice and the acoustics of my room enhanced her talents. One night the bombing was close and they all huddled together in terror and in the morning they discovered that their grandmother had died in the night. I had seen her soul move up through my branches just after midnight and I bade her farewell. Her son decided to bury her beside me and now she keeps me company as I can often hear her sweet singing in my leaves.

In the 16th-century my shelter was occupied by a healer although many called her a witch. Many of the locals called on her for medicinal remedies to cure mild ailments like coughs and colds and stomach problems. She also helped women with the means to prevent pregnancies by the use of herbal remedies as she knew that another mouth to feed would cause problems for the family. Sometimes she was asked for love potions when a man or woman did not feel that their feelings were being reciprocated and many of the ladies of the great houses would consult her on such matters. However one day a group of men dragged her away after a remedy had not worked and a man had died. She could never have cured him as his body was riddled with tumours so he was wasting away but she was blamed and burned at the stake. Fortunately a fellow healer bribed her jailer to provide a large dose of hemlock to take before she was led out so her pain was lessened as she was barely conscious.

In medieval times the peasants who lived in the village would come and sit beneath my branches in the summer months on the odd occasions when they had some free time. They had a hard life working all day on the nearby farms owned by nobles. They tended to keep their own cows and would sometimes lead them to graze around the tree where the grass grew lush. They relied on the dairy produce to survive making buttermilk, cheese and curds and whey, although most of the time they ate a dish called pottage, a thick soup containing meat, vegetables, or bran.

A regular visitor with her cow was a young girl with a club foot whose parents sent her away during busy times like harvest as she was unable to work as hard as the others thereby affecting their joint family wages. She used to sit and make daisy chains and talk to me about her family worries albeit that she did not know that I could hear and understand her. But I think that it gave her some comfort and she was able to express all her feelings and concerns without fear of being ridiculed. I grew fond of her but like all my visitors she only stayed for a short period of time in comparison to my lifetime. She was eventually taken by the plague as were all her family but in the meantime she had been happily married to an older man with three children who was not bothered about her disability.

Of course it is not just humans who have been grateful for the shelter that I have provided over the years and I have lost count of the many creatures that I have housed and continue to do so – squirrels, birds of varying species, many different insects and varieties of fungi. Mistletoe grows in my boughs and ivy climbs from my base. Lately a pair of parakeets have taken up residence and it is interesting to hear them calling to each other in the woodland. They are not a native species and are regarded as a pest in some areas of London where their numbers have multiplied but I like them as their colourful plumage of red, pink and lime green brightens my day.

I do not know how much longer I will live in my woodland as I have not been feeling myself lately. I have seen a dark fluid oozing from my splits in my bark from a metre above the ground and above. There was another oak tree a mile or so away that died a few years ago whose symptoms started as mine have who sent me a message through my creature friends to say goodbye and tell me that she had a disease of oak trees which is caused by a bacterial infection. I understand that death comes fairly quickly within five years so I must ensure that I warn all my residents that their accommodation may be short-lived so that they can make preparations. But at least I know that I have left many children to continue my line as my acorns have germinated throughout the wood and although in most cases it will be many years before they achieve my longevity there are already some who are a few hundred years old so I will live on through them.

LIFE IS A LOTTERY

Linda H

John Parker watched the plastic bag as it floated, inches above him. It seemed undecided whether it should remain there hovering or head for pastures new. A sudden gust of wind made the decision, and blew it in front of John's face. He reached his hand up to protect his face, just as it started to rain, and the handle caught around his little finger.

'Well', thought John, 'It's an ill wind that blows nobody any good'. The rain was coming down now, and what better way to protect his library books, than with a captured plastic bag.

John went to the library most days as it was lovely and warm in there. This was much appreciated by a pensioner, rich in time but poor in pocket.

Mary Collins smiled warmly as John approached the returns desk with his books. John enjoyed his chats with Mary. She was a font of all knowledge. The transaction completed, he made his way to the reading room to chinwag with his friends. He spotted Bill and Frank sitting at a desk. John coughed quietly and both men looked up. Whispered greetings were exchanged.

Later, when he returned home, John took his new books out of the carrier bag and put them on the table. But, to his surprise, there was a piece of paper on the bottom of the bag. Due to its orangey/pink colour, he knew exactly what it was: a lottery ticket.

He looked at the date and realised it was for that evening's draw. Wouldn't it be wonderful if this ticket – thrown his way by fate – turned out to be a winner?

Meanwhile, a few streets away, Gemma Collins was at a loss to know how to help her mum, Mary. 'I'm sure it'll turn up. Can you remember if you put it in your purse or your shopping bag?'

Mary gave a sigh, 'I'm not sure. I rushed into the supermarket after I left the library, it was so busy at the checkout and my shopping bag wasn't big enough, so I asked for a plastic bag – cost me an extra five pence, that did. And, before you ask, I didn't get a chance to check the carrier bag'.

Gemma was puzzled. 'Well, it's simple really dear', her mum said. 'The vegetable rack is just inside the back door. I took the potatoes out of the carrier bag and put them in the rack, but before I had a chance to close the door, the bag was caught by a gust of wind, and flew away.'

'Oh, mum, problem solved. If you've looked everywhere else, it must be in the carrier bag. Why don't you just go and buy another ticket, in case it wins. You choose the same numbers every week. 7 for luck. 16 from your favourite song, Sweet Sixteen. 23 and 12 for dad's birthday and 31 and 3 for mine.'

But, as they looked at the clock, they realised it was gone seven o'clock, and the shop was closed now.

Meanwhile John had gone to the Red Lion to meet Bill and Frank for a pint. As he walked in, Bill stopped looking at the large screen TV above the bar, 'The lottery is just starting. Has anyone been daft enough to buy a ticket?'

'Funny you should ask that', said John, 'The strangest thing happened earlier today.'

Bill and Frank sat open mouthed as he told them the story of the plastic bag. Bill, who was still amazed at the story, started to read the numbers out as they appeared on the screen.

If they had been surprised at John's story, that was nothing compared to the stunned realisation that the ticket was a match: five numbers plus the Bonus Ball!

'Heavens, John, you've just won half a million quid, I think it's your round.'

John was silent for a few minutes, then he took a deep breath. 'I can't cash that ticket, it isn't mine. Whoever bought it could be a pensioner just like us. They could be struggling to make ends meet. It would be stealing. There must be a way to find out who bought it'.

He decided he would go to the library on Monday, and ask Mary. If there was a way, she was bound to know.

Monday morning, first thing, he was at the library.

'Morning John. You look as though you've lost a pound and found a penny.'

John smiled at the joke. 'I need to ask your advice'.

'Ask away.'

'If I wanted to find out who had bought a lottery ticket, how would I go about it.'

'Em, well, contacting the lottery administrators might be a start. They can tell where and when a ticket was bought, but I don't think they can tell you exactly who bought it, Why do you ask?'

John told her the whole story. But her reaction was a surprise. She rushed around the desk and gave him a big hug.

Later that evening, Gemma repeated the embrace. Also hugging Frank and Bill, who had tagged along to bask in the glory.

It was soon agreed that the prize would be shared equally between the two of them. After all, a quarter of a million pounds was still a lot of money!

It wasn't until they were all sat down with a glass of port, that Mary finally looked at the ticket, and she let out a scream. 'This isn't my ticket. This was bought at a different shop. We can't cash this ticket, it would be like stealing'.

For a moment or two, the whole room was silent . . . Then everyone burst out laughing.

ONE ARABIAN NIGHT

Mary

Evelyn awoke with a start as if from a dream, one of those where she was running, her heart pounding, running from something unknown, running as fast as she could but was getting nowhere.

The bedroom felt different. It was stiflingly hot which made no sense as when she had finally let sleep engulf her in the bedroom with the beamed ceiling in the cosy cottage in rural Cornwall she shared with her husband and two cats, it had been a cold clear winter's night, moonlight dancing on the covering of snow which gave the appearance that the world had been sprinkled with glitter.

This wasn't her bedroom. Where was she and how did she get here? A feeling of panic began to engulf her. Had aliens visited and spirited her away? There had been talk in the village about strange lights in the night sky but this had been started by Oliver and he was 'away with the fairies' as her husband so quaintly put it and no one took him seriously.

She looked around the room, the window was in the wrong place and it was open to let in what little movement of air there was and also the sounds and smells of the street, unfamiliar cries in a language she didn't understand. She got out of bed only it wasn't a bed, merely a pallet on the floor, the wooden floorboards rough beneath her bare feet. She went to the window and on looking out saw the house was perched on the pink terracotta walls of an ancient city, a lazy sea lapped the rocks at the base of the walls. Where was she and why? The landscape reminded her of a long ago holiday taken in North Africa.

She turned and looked around the room noting how sparsely furnished it was, just a couple of what appeared to be chests or blanket boxes and a single uncomfortable looking stool as well as the pallet.

Running to the door her only thought was I have got to get out of here. The door was locked, she tried the handle again and again but the door wouldn't budge, she kicked the door, she shouted again and again – nothing. Could she climb out of the window and escape that way? No, it was a sheer drop onto the rocks.

Despair took over. What was going on? She heard the sound of a key in the lock. Suddenly the door crashed open to reveal the silhouette of tall robed figure. The figure threw a bundle of material at Evelyn, said something unintelligible pointing first at Evelyn then the bundle. From this Evelyn supposed she was to put on whatever it was.

The robed figure turned to leave. 'Wait', she cried, 'Where am I and who are you?' The figure did not reply but left locking the door behind him.

She looked at the bundle of material on the floor, picked it up and shook out the contents. It appeared to consist of wide trousers loosely gathered at the waist and ankles, harem pants she thought, a sequin-encrusted cropped top and a filmy veil again edged with sequins. A belly-dancer's costume she surmised. Was she about to be whisked away to join a Sultan's harem?

Some years ago she and a friend did a class to learn the art of the dance as a joke so at least she knew how to wear the costume. She was in two minds about changing, what would happen if she didn't and what would happen if she did? She took off her cosy comfy PJs and put on the filmy garments.

The door opened again to reveal the same robed figure, he came into the room and roughly took Evelyn's arm and almost dragged her out. Once outside she could see a richly decorated building opposite where she had found herself. The walls were covered in beautiful mosaic tiles in rich turquoise blues, navy and terracotta. A small brown cat sat outside, it looked like Evelyn's cats and the thought of not seeing them or her beloved husband again brought huge wracking sobs. The tall man shook her roughly hissing something she didn't understand. He took her towards the lavishly decorated building and pushed her through a small door in the wall. She found herself in a large courtyard filled with every kind of exotic plant imaginable, all in ornately carved pots. Her robed escort walked her towards the far end of the courtyard to a pair of imposing carved wooden doors standing some fifteen feet high. A small wicket door opened in one of the doors and a veiled woman beckoned her inside. Her escort pushed her inside closing the door behind her.

Evelyn looked around the brightly-lit room at the sea of people. The veiled woman who opened the door took her hand and guided her around the outside of the room to a small door which she opened to reveal an area which seemed to be a waiting room for dancers. There was silence in the room together with an air of apprehension that was almost palpable.

A drum sounded nearby which must have been a signal as the veiled woman arranged the dancers in a long line placing Evelyn towards the end of it. A further drum roll sounded, the door opened and the dancers began to file out into the main room. Music started and the girls began their routine, Evelyn copying the dancers next to her. The routine had been in progress for what seemed like hours to Evelyn but in reality it was five or six minutes.

Suddenly members of the predominately male audience leapt to their feet approached the girls and started to drag individuals away. A man came up to Evelyn, she thought he looked rather like her husband but his eyes were cold and his face had a cruel twist. He grabbed her arm tightly and pulled her towards some wall hangings that she had not noticed before, she tried to resist but he was far too strong. Evelyn had never been so frightened. What fate awaited her behind those wall hangings? She screamed.

Suddenly it seemed as though the room was shaking, Evelyn was aware of a familiar voice calling her name softly at first, 'Evie, Evie', then more insistently, 'Evie, Evie, wake up'.

CAROLINE VISITS MARRAKECH

Lynda A

Leila's friend Caroline had flown over to Spain to avoid some of the awful weather England suffers in January and also to help her move some of her belongings from Spain to Marrakech where she had recently bought and renovated a riad.

She had collected her from Malaga airport and, as was her wont, her friend had talked non-stop from leaving the airport to arriving at her little house in the heart of Estepona village.

They had spent a couple of pleasant days together wandering around Estepona, having meals in the warm sunshine and gloating about how their friends in England would not be doing the same, watching the fishing boats going out and returning and marvelling at the colours as the sun set over the calm Mediterranean.

The journey from Estepona to Marrakech was also filled with her friend's chat . . . it really seemed like she never ran out of things to talk about; the journey took nearly ten hours, which is a lot of talking.

So, had she been consulted about her friend's health and wellbeing, she would have sighed, rolled her eyes and said she was her usual, ebullient self.

Unfortunately the same could not have been said for the following day; Caroline woke up feeling distinctly under the weather and decided to stay in bed for the day. Leila's husband, Hamed, said he would look after all her needs whilst Leila carried out the various bureaucratic necessities for opening their riad.

After racing around to the various offices she returned to the riad hoping for lunch and a bit of peace and quiet, but she was met by a very distraught Hamed.

'I think Caroline is dead!' He blurted out with a look of absolute terror plastered on his face, 'I went to her room with some lunch and thought she was just asleep; but when I touched her face to wake her up it was stone cold. Please go and have a look . . . I can't go back in there again'.

In trepidation she went to Caroline's room and knocked on the door; there was no answer. She walked over to her friend's prostrate form and gave her shoulder a shake; Caroline's hand flopped lifelessly against the bed. She gave a silent scream (probably best in the Medina where everybody hears each other's business) then tucked her friend in, went back out and shut the door.

She and Hamed sat in the patio in silence both with a coffee and cigarette; even though Hamed had stopped smoking months previously, today he felt the need of the psychological sustenance it would provide.

'I think the thing to do would be to phone the British Consulate and ask them what we should do' suggested Leila, 'If anyone should know it will be them'.

'Don't call the police!' is all Hamed kept saying.

She found the number of the Consulate and dialled it but was met with a voice message, *The Consulate is shut for the weekend; in cases of emergency call the British Embassy on . . .*

She dialled the number given only to be greeted with the same message but with the suggestion to contact the Consulate in cases of emergency.

'Well that's no help at all!' she grumbled to Hamed.

'Don't call the police', he countered.

She then Googled, *What to do if a non-Muslim tourist dies in a Muslim country* which also proved no help at all, it just gave a lot of history of how Muslims bury their dead and why.

'We can't report it to the authorities', Hamed told her, 'They will put us in prison; they won't believe she just died, they will say we killed her'.

'So what do you suggest we do?' This was greeted with a shrug.

'Let's go for a walk; a nice long walk will help us clear our brains, then we'll stop at the Tazi and have a beer. Then we will decide what to do.' Leila always found walking helped, especially a long, fast walk; Hamed just wanted not to be left alone in the riad with Caroline.

So they walked all around the old walls of the city; they walked in silence with Leila wracking her brains about how to deal with this catastrophe and Hamed wishing he had never been born, or at least that Caroline had never come to Morocco . . . why could she not have died at home like normal people.

After a couple of beers each at the Tazi they returned to the riad where Hamed looked in askance at Leila as soon as they sat down . . . she tended to be the problem solver.

'Right', she said, 'As far as I know Caroline has no family, so nobody will miss her in the near future anyway. We need to cover our backs if, as you say, the police will not believe that she died naturally and will think we killed her . . . I don't want to go to prison either. I think we need to get rid of the evidence'.

'So, as I imagine she would want to be cremated, we will do just that.'

'What is cremated?' It was a word Hamed had not come across in English.

'Burned. We must make a fire and burn her body.'

He looked at her in stunned silence; it was a concept he hadn't encountered before either and it left him aghast.

'It's Eid tomorrow so everyone will be chopping up their sheep and burning the wool off the heads. We will do the same but with Caroline. We'll need a big metal dustbin to contain the fire so I need you to go out and get the biggest one you can find and lots of firewood.'

Hamed looked at her with incredulity; was this really his wife suggesting such an abomination?

'Look, if you have any better ideas then please share them', she said, 'If not, then please go and buy what I just told you we need; and make sure you get lots of firewood from different places, we don't want people asking awkward questions'.

He picked up the car keys and scuttled out of the door with a look of total panic in his eyes; it would hopefully be easier just to do the shopping and leave the grisly bits to Leila. She, meanwhile, went around Caroline's room and collected everything that could suggest she had even visited the riad; all her clothes, shoes, books, a pharmacy of pills and her passport . . . all these things would hopefully help the fire burn nice and hot.

Hamed made several journeys with a car full of wood until she felt they would have enough, or hoped they would have enough; he had also found a large metal dustbin.

'Well I think we've done all we can for now', stated Leila, 'Let's get some dinner out, I don't really feel up to cooking this evening'. Hamed agreed, but deep down he was wondering how she could even consider eating at a time like this . . . how could she be so matter of fact; why was she not feeling the fear that he was experiencing; would he ever be able to look at her in the same way again, knowing what she was capable of organising.

They ate a little and then spent the night both tossing and turning; agitated by visions of what the following day would bring and how it would all work out.

The following day saw them building a base to the dustbin so the heat would not spoil the Zellige tiles and putting enough kindling inside to start the fire. They then had to wait, along with all the other inhabitants of the Medina, for the alert that the king had slaughtered his sheep so they could all follow suit. At last there would be a good use for the sword that had appeared randomly one day in a cupboard; Leila hoped it would be sharp enough.

Once the horn had sounded, they went together to Caroline's room, Leila feeling very grateful that they had put her in the bedroom which opened directly onto the patio; noise carried less at ground floor level and it would be easier to move her to her funeral pyre. What a shame they couldn't just build a big fire, like they would in India, onto which they could lay her intact and cremate her with more dignity.

But that was not to be; she was too big to put into the dustbin whole.

'Help me get her out of bed onto the floor', she instructed Hamed who, by now, understood it would be best to do as he was told, especially once he had noticed the sword by the door. They laid her on top of an old sleeping bag.

'I think if we chop off her arms and legs we should be able to burn the rest of her whole', said Leila, 'Can you do that while I start the fire?'

'Hamed?'

Then she realised that her husband was cowering by the door with an expression of abject terror written on every pore of his face.

'OK, you go and get the fire started please. I'll have to do the butchery myself.'

He went out into the patio and she shut the door.

Before Leila started she apologised to her old friend, sure that she would understand, that in other circumstances they would actually have a good laugh about it; she then said a quick prayer asking God to accept a new entrant.

She then inspected where she should make the initial chop, lifted the sword, closed her eyes and brought down the sword with all her strength. Luckily it was very sharp and within minutes she had cut off both arms and legs. She then lifted the first arm and took it out to the fire that was, by now, burning quite brightly and hot. She passed it to Hamed and went back into the room for its partner. When she came back out Hamed had laid it over the top of the fire; that would not do.

'No Hamed, if you do that you are just cooking her. We don't want her cooked, we need her turned to ashes', and with that she pushed the arm into the fire itself accompanied by its partner. These were soon followed by the two legs and Caroline's luggage then left to burn for a while until there was room for more.

By nightfall the cadaver was no more; it had been joined by the soiled sleeping bag and everything had been reduced to ashes. Leila had a quick look around the riad for any evidence that her friend had ever been there.

Only then did she allow herself to weaken; she sat down and cried . . . partly out of sadness for the loss of her friend, partly out of relief that it was all over and she would never have to do such an awful thing again. Hamed joined her in her tears.

They decided to spend that night in a hotel; neither of them felt they could sleep at the scene of carnage.

They realised that sooner or later someone would wonder what had happened to Caroline; her neighbours in England would probably know that she had intended to visit Marrakech with Leila; the police would know that she had entered Morocco owing to the individual number everyone entering had stamped in their passports. Sooner or later the British police would start investigating.

The following day they went back to the riad, scooped the ashes into a pot and cleared up everything else; they threw the dustbin into the old riad next door that nobody lived in or ever visited. Then they packed up all their own personal belongings and put them in the car. The final thing they did in Marrakech was to visit an estate agents to put the riad on the market; they were assured that everything could be done online; all they had to do was leave the keys and keep in touch via email. On the way across the Mediterranean they emptied her ashes into the sea, then neatly put the pot into a rubbish container.

Six months later sees them living in Santa Marta in Colombia; the riad had sold quickly as it had been newly renovated and pristine, the money had been sent to Leila's account in Spain where they had lived whilst waiting for the sale to go through. As soon as it was all sorted out they moved to Colombia, took on assumed names, and opened a hotel there.

Hamed (now Miguel) could never look at Leila (now Maria) in the same way, now he knew what she was capable of, but it was safer to stay with her than try to go back home.

THE VOICE

Bryony

The first time was in Trafalgar Square. Sarah had heard a voice – crystal clear like spring water falling over rocks – almost childlike it its pitch so she was unable to tell whether it was a young boy or a girl's voice.

'You have been chosen', the voice said. Sarah looked around her but could see no one near enough to have spoken to her. She was confused but in the end she put it down to the acoustics in the area. The next time that Sarah heard the voice she was shopping in her local market on a Saturday afternoon.

This time the voice said, 'You are the first of many'. She looked around her but again was unable to see anyone who might have spoken. She was beginning to wonder if she was hallucinating as a result of the tragedies that she had experienced over the past few months. As she started to walk home she wasn't looking where she was going and bumped into a tall blonde man. As she apologised she noticed that he had unusual coloured eyes that were almost turquoise – then she felt herself being drawn into a kind of void by the eyes as if she was in a blue fluorescent bubble. He pulled her close to him and she felt a jolt like lightning pass between them. She must have passed out as the next thing that she remembered was being helped up by a passer by who said that she had seen her fall. Sarah asked whether the man that she had collided with was alright but the woman said that she hadn't seen anyone near her when she fell. She thanked the woman for her help, and then made her way home.

When she got back to her flat Sarah felt incredibly tired so after putting away her shopping she laid on the settee for a quick nap and quickly fell asleep. However she didn't wake until the next morning when she felt ravenous – but much refreshed. She was full of energy and happy to be alive which was so different to how she had been feeling recently. Sarah's husband had been in the army and was killed abroad on active service leaving her pregnant. She had carried the child full term but he had been stillborn. She could remember every detail of his sweet face and tiny hands with an almost star-shaped birthmark on the inside of his right wrist. She remembered kissing it, and then she held him for a few hours afterwards until the nurse took him from her.

The next few months passed without incident. Everyone kept telling her how well she looked – quite radiant – and she could see the change in herself when she looked in the mirror. Recalling her long exhausted sleep on that Saturday she decided that the voice and the long sleep had been the turning point in her recovery from the trauma of the loss of her husband and child, and now she felt positive about moving forward with her life. The only thing that she found annoying was that she had been gaining weight and although her appetite had improved she didn't feel that such a large increase in her waist size was justified. One of her friends had even asked her if she was pregnant again. Sarah knew that this definitely couldn't be the case but she wondered if she was having a phantom pregnancy in view of the hormone problems she experienced after the loss of her child, so she made an appointment with her GP.

Sarah explained her concerns to the GP who examined her and said, 'This is not a phantom pregnancy but I would estimate that you are around five months pregnant'.

'That's impossible', said Sarah, 'I haven't had sex with anyone since my husband died'. The GP looked at her quizzically and Sarah felt that he didn't believe her.

'Well you are overdue for your first scan so I will get you an urgent appointment and then you will be able to see for yourself.'

The appointment was made for the next week and Sarah was confident that it would show that she was right but she was now concerned that it would show a tumour or something worse in her womb.

'There you are Sarah – here's the baby on the screen', said the nurse, 'Do you want to know the sex?'

Sarah looked at the screen and could clearly see a baby but there appeared to be something wrong with the screen as the baby was glowing blue. She asked why but the nurse said that she couldn't see anything wrong with it, and that perhaps Sarah ought to get a sight test if she was seeing colours. She told Sarah that she was having a boy. Sarah thought that she was going mad. Perhaps she had had some sort of memory loss and had intercourse with someone – but who?

The pregnancy passed normally and the voice kept reassuring her throughout that everything was progressing well. She began to look forward to hearing it and experienced a deep sense of wellbeing after each contact made. But Sarah didn't tell anyone about the voice in case they thought she was losing her mind, and would be an unfit mother and take her child away from her.

When her labour started the voice said, 'Not long now – all will be well'.

Sarah gave birth to a healthy boy with no complications, but when she was alone in her room and took the child to her she noticed that his eyes were bright turquoise and that his skin looked fluorescent. 'I really must get my eyes tested', she thought.

She had named the boy after her late husband but when she put him back in his cot and laid back to try to sleep the voice came again.

'You cannot name this child as he is not yours and we must take him. You have done well and your reward will be greater than you can ever imagine.'

Sarah awoke screaming, 'No – don't take my baby'. The nurse who came to see what was the matter said that she must have had a bad dream as her baby was fine. But when she looked into the cot she did not see the child that she had just given birth to but the son that she had buried. She lifted his tiny hand and saw the star shaped birthmark on the inside of his right wrist – this was definitely him.

Sarah never heard the voice again and told no one about her experience. But she hoped that wherever he was her other child was thriving and happy.

LEICESTER SQUARE

Linda H

I don't know what made me decide to tidy out the loft, today of all days. We were moving house soon, and it needed to be done, but it was a chore I had been putting it off. However, I soon became engrossed in sorting out all my old photos, documents and even my old teenage diaries.

I picked up one of my diaries and it fell open, so I started to read it and it brought back such memories, as I used to write in it every day. I wrote as if I was having a conversation with one of my friends. Soon I was engrossed and was smiling away to myself.

I don't know what had made me pick the one from 1993, perhaps it was fate. I decided I had time to read a few pages. So I pulled up a tea chest and began.

Dear Diary,

I met someone today, I know what you are going to say. Not again. But, Yes, this again! Meeting someone new, getting to know them better than they know themselves. Falling in love with them because of the silliest reasons, and the vicious dating cycle continues.

Nevertheless, like every other time, I'll say, I think he is THE ONE. You will silently roll your eyes at me because this is like the twelfth THE ONE. I'll pretend not to notice, when deep down, even I know it will probably fail again. But, at least I've still got this magical feeling called HOPE.

So, more about this guy, and about today. I have known him for a few months, but it was only today that we actually spoke. He's one of the librarians at my local library that I visit every week. We used to exchange, 'Hi.

Taking Books out or returning this week', or, 'Thanks, Bye.'

But, yesterday, he was stocking the shelves, and we got to talking, and it turns out we have a lot in common. He knows my taste in books. So when he asked me out on a date, he did so by quoting one of the characters from my favourite author, Dickens. I thought that was a cue, so I went ahead and said Yes!

We arranged to meet at my usual *First Date* restaurant. Chosen by me as it was close to where I lived. Also, it was close to the tube station and Leicester Square. So, if the date didn't work out, and I didn't want my date to know that I lived two minutes away in Charing Cross Road, then I could pretend to be catching the underground.

It was a great date. We talked and ate and laughed. The dinner went smoothly, with each of us asking the questions we had obviously researched. Mine came from a book that I had actually bought, *What to do and what not to do on a first date.*

Anyway, we got to know quite a bit about each other. But we really got to know each other properly when we left the restaurant and went for a walk.

We walked around Leicester Square, then cut down one of the side streets. It was just perfect at that time of night. Not too crowded, and not too lonely. We just talked and talked, but then we both fell silent at the same time, just enjoying the moment. But he didn't need to ask me whether I was fine or if there was anything bothering me. Just by looking at me, he knew I was happy in that moment.

As we walked, almost touching, our hands became attracted to each other like magnets. Our hands knowingly and flirtatiously touched until finally, we kissed.

Our first kiss in that perfect moment. It didn't feel like any of the other firsts. It was truly magic.

So, all in all, diary, a pretty perfect first date.

I was still smiling as I flicked through the other pages, Our second date, again at Leicester Square, this time to get tickets for a show. Later on that year, our engagement. Then a Christmas wedding.

Suddenly, my mind came back to the present, and I realised the time. I hadn't left myself much time to get ready. Chris would be home soon, and we had to be at the restaurant by 7.30. Back where we first met. My first date restaurant. But I never had another first date. Just a second, third, twentieth. We were meeting our family there to celebrate our silver wedding anniversary.

So our story really did have a happy ending.

WAS THAT REALLY ME?

Mary

It was a beautiful autumn morning, the sun shining in an almost cloudless blue sky, it if wasn't for the chilly breeze one could almost imagine it was July. The leaves were wearing their autumn colours, yellow, orange, russet and many shades of brown from tan and beige through to deep, deep chocolate, not forgetting the acers resplendent in their coat of dappled red.

Louise was taking her much loved labrador Ellie on her favourite walk through the cemetery on the local common. At this time of year the fallen leaves gave Ellie hours of fun as she chased through them. Louise loved walking through the dry leaves, scuffling them up causing a very satisfying crunching noise as she did so.

Ellie was off her lead and away running through the leaves. Louise wandered along enjoying the peace and solitude as the majority of walkers seemed to avoid the cemetery. Suddenly the peace was shattered by prolonged barking. Louise knew that bark, it was Ellie who was nowhere in sight. As she turned a corner she could see Ellie standing looking at something on the ground and barking madly. As she drew closer Louise could see that it was a shoe, on closer inspection, the right half of a pair of expensive black patent leather men's dress shoes just sitting in the middle of the path in a state of total abandonment.

How on earth had it got there? Had the wearer been passing through in the dead of night and been spooked by something and fled in a panic too frightened to return for their shoe? After all it was Halloween. Or had they been up to no good? Louise had heard the many stories of goings on in that cemetery.

Louise decided to take the shoe with her thinking that perhaps she could reunite it with its owner. But before setting off on her quest Louise sat down on one of many seats in a sheltered spot away from the breeze to plan how best to go about this. As she sat letting the warmth of the sun and peaceful surroundings engulf her the trees dissolved, morphing into what appeared to be an expensively-decorated dining room or restaurant resplendent with crystal chandeliers, crisp white linen tablecloths, sparkling glassware and cutlery precisely placed. The room was full of the rise and fall of muted conversation, the chink of cutlery against porcelain as deferential waiters hovered. Louise felt a sensation of floating above it.

All of the tables were occupied. A distinguished looking mixed-race man accompanied by a beautiful young woman were seated at a table towards the front of the room just to the left of the entrance. They looked rather uncomfortable, their eyes following the waiters' every move almost as if they were waiting for a signal or planning something.

With a shock Louise recognised the woman as her younger self and the man as a shady figure from her past with whom she had had an intense relationship. He was mad, bad and dangerous to know leading her into his dissolute world. What was happening? Why was she watching that scenario playing out before her and why?

She remembered how alive she felt during their exploits and being young didn't think of repercussions. She knew he was a hustler and that it was wrong in every sense of the word but she had to admit the buzz from the adrenalin was more than enough to push any doubts out of her mind. Life was one round of madness, darting from one escapade to the next and staying just one step ahead from being caught.

Louise watched as the evening progressed. She didn't remember this particular occasion although to be fair as she got older she thought about this part of her past less and less feeling a sense of embarrassment, shame and horror that she could have been involved in something so heinous.

As she watched, her younger self and her companion rose from the table and walked towards the door. Their waiter, suddenly aware of their intention to avoid paying the bill hurried towards them calling, 'Sir, madam'. On hearing this they sprinted towards the door and out into the street, running fast they diverted into an alleyway where they collapsed against each other laughing. It wasn't that they couldn't pay as previous exploits had netted rich pickings but where was the thrill in that? As their breathing returned to normal Louise noticed her partner in crime was minus a shoe, a black patent leather dress shoe.

The scene gradually faded away and Louise was aware of trees around her, the sun had gone and she was cold and could feel Ellie's cold nose against her hand. Had that just happened she asked herself remembering that when she sat down she had with her the shoe which she intended to try and return to its rightful owner. Was her possession of the shoe responsible for the flashback to that time? If that was the case she thought trying to find the owner was perhaps not such a good idea. She got up and threw the shoe as hard and as far as she possibly could into the trees, Ellie darted off to retrieve it. Louise called her back putting her on her lead before turning towards home and quickening her pace.

In the meantime not far away in The Café on The Common a well-dressed mixed race man ordered espresso. He looked out of place in his expensive suit amongst the other customers in their warm fleeces and sensible walking boots. Something else made him conspicuous – he was wearing one shoe, an expensive black patent leather dress shoe.

CECILIA

Lynda A

Cecilia was born in Medellin, Colombia, the only child of local drug baron Jose Ortega and his wife Paola. As their only offspring, and a daughter to boot, she was spoiled rotten by her parents . . . nothing was too good for their little princess.

As Jose's empire grew, they moved from the apartment they occupied in Medellin to a villa he had had built to his specifications in the sleepy village of Puerto Colombia. Many of his mafiosi associates lived in nearby Barranquilla, but he thought their lives would be safer in the villa which was situated on a dirt road surrounded by locally-owned bungalows . . . it was the kind of road where cows roamed at their leisure and dogs barked at any approaching traffic, of which there was very little. The villa was surrounded by a ten-foot wall topped with broken glass and contained most of the necessities of their day-to-day, including a swimming pool, maids' quarters and running water (which most of the houses on the street lacked . . . their water coming through a pipe in the gardens every five days or so).

Thus, from the age of six until her seventeenth birthday, Cecilia spent her days ensconced behind high walls being taught by a private tutor who came daily from Barranquilla, along with the odd play dates with her friends' and relatives' offspring. They had, of course, the occasional holiday in Miami . . . where they spent the days in a high-security holiday compound socialising with other mafiosi families. There was also the annual trip to Paris, Milan or London to attend fashion shows and update their already extensive wardrobes.

As you can see she led a very sheltered and pampered life.

Suddenly, at the age of seventeen, her world disintegrated. Her parents, on their way back home from a meeting with other mafiosi drug barons in Barranquilla were gunned down (the car received a full round of bullets from a machine gun . . . killing all the occupants of the car, including the driver); their heads were hacked off with machetes then placed on spikes by the side of the road as a warning; their bodies left for the wild dogs to devour.

Cecilia was the sole heir to her father's immense fortune (and drug empire).

Once it became common knowledge amongst the mafia clans that the Ortega family had been slaughtered, whole families descended on Puerto Colombia to attend the funeral of *two of theirs*. Soon after, Cecilia found herself inundated with mafia solicitors wanting to give advice, also young, up-and-coming mafia studs wanting marriage and a stake in the empire she had inherited along with the fortune. Surrounded by all this attention Cecilia had never felt so alone.

She realised she had to make a quick decision before she became too embroiled in the whole mafia scenario. She made up her mind that she would go to Miami where she could be incognito as long as she stayed away from the mafia holiday compounds; she would rent an apartment by the beach where she would try to get her head round what had happened to her and make a plan for her future; it would be scary being alone, but possibly less frightening than being besieged by the mafia clans.

For the first time in her sheltered life Cecilia packed her bags, informed the staff that she was going away for a while but would continue to pay their wages; she emptied her father's safe and took a taxi into Barranquilla where she stayed for one night at the Majestic Hotel (using her false passport under the name of Francesca Ortiz; they had always used fake passports to hide their movements from mafia rivals).

The next morning, having consumed her favourite breakfast of *arepa con huevo* accompanied by a fresh maracuya juice, she quickly vacated her room and hailed her own taxi to the airport . . . just in case. It was simple to get a first-class ticket to Miami, there were always spare seats. Once through the police checks and customs there was only an hour's wait; then just two and a half hours later they landed at Miami airport. And what a different experience from what she was used to on arriving in her father's private jet. The air conditioning was not working so it was stifling, the airport was full of travellers racing here and there with no regard to other people . . . several times she was pushed aside. The police check felt like an ignominy when they asked her reason for visiting the United States . . . suggesting she was there to work illegally, perhaps as a maid. At this point her mafiosi mindset kicked in when she felt the word *revenge* stick in her throat. But she managed to smile her way through all of this humiliation and somehow found herself the other side of the police check. Customs was much easier, she only had one bag (albeit one bag full to the brim with money) and the confident walk of an innocent woman with nothing to hide . . . she walked straight through the *Nothing to Declare* section out into the sauna that is Miami.

Joining the taxi queue she thought the best thing to do was to get to the Metropolitan Hotel which she had seen advertised in the airport and then walk a little to find a different hotel. She discovered *The Betsy* quite easily and they had a 'Superior Suite' vacant for two weeks; this was useful in that the balcony overlooked the pool and not the road . . . less likely she could be spotted by anyone not staying at the hotel, anyone who might wish her harm.

That week was a week of fun for her; she had her hair cut and styled in a different way, then she shopped until she dropped three days running, buying the kind of clothes she would never have been allowed to buy had her parents been with her. She then realised she should make a concentrated effort to find an apartment but she had no experience in such matters and therefore no idea how to find one. Who to ask? Who to trust? Eventually she asked Carolina, the receptionist at the hotel, who had always seemed very pleasant . . . good choice. It was her day off the next day and she offered to go to a real estate agency with her. Accordingly the following day they went to several agencies and collecting an armful of details . . . she didn't want her new friend to know which she would choose, she must still be very careful.

Two weeks after her arrival at the hotel she left as quickly and quietly as possible during Carolina's lunch break (leaving her nonetheless a thank you note and some money), getting her own taxi once she was in the street. She was soon installed in the apartment she had rented for the next six months . . . it was furnished so the only thing she had to do was unpack all her new clothes.

Every day she made forays into the various districts of Miami, with each passing day feeling more confident and more at ease. The only problem she encountered every time was the fact that she was so obviously South American. Americans thought she was an illegal immigrant and as such disdained her; others of her race were much more welcoming, but perhaps overly so.

In order to fit in better she had to devise another plan. She wrote a list of possible changes she could make to her appearance

Dye her hair blonde.

Lose weight . . . she was quite large compared to the skinny people she saw on South Beach.

Get her eyebrows plucked to a fine line.

Have skin-lightening procedure.

All of these things were achievable and so she started on her transformation. Within a few days she was blonde with very fine eyebrows (the remainder of which had had to be bleached in order to match her hair. She had been to a dietician who had given her a strict diet sheet which she knew she would follow religiously. She had also found a beauty parlour which specialised in skin-lightening and had had her first treatment.

Things were definitely looking up but she was also lonely, she was used to having company every day. She spoke to people in the shops but she wanted relationships more intimate than casual, someone she could speak to about her life, who she could share things with.

Almost as if the gods were inside her mind she found a flyer in her mailbox offering a meeting up of new residents to Miami; the venue was a smart café nearby, the first meeting the following Saturday.

With more than a little trepidation she arrived at the venue at the allotted time. There she met up with a lot of people of all ages and nationalities, it was all so easy . . . everyone desperate to make friends in their adopted city, she wasn't alone in this. She found herself at a table with a lovely group of girls, all just accepting each other . . . no awkward questions asked. They agreed to meet up independently the following Saturday for lunch.

They soon became quite a clique who met regularly for coffee, lunch, shopping trips and for girly nights in. She found that most of them were there in the hope of becoming models or meeting a rich husband; some of them had tried in LA but found the place too daunting . . . the competition too hard. They had all undergone at least one plastic surgery procedure, were considering more, in the quest for perfection.

Cecilia began to study her appearance more critically; she had lost a lot of weight, her hair was looking more natural now her skin was lightening, but could she . . . should she be doing more? This question was discussed at one of their lunch meetings and the consensus of opinion was that she should try some of the less invasive treatments available as a taster; so the following week saw her accompany one of her friends to see Ignatio Munez who was one of the best plastic surgeons in Miami. He suggested she try a little botox as a starter, followed by lip augmentation; he was the professional, she followed his proposal and was happy with the results.

What next she wondered . . . this was fun.

She thought perhaps her face lacked definition so went back, on her own, to see Ignatio again. He told her she could have cheek augmentation to give her the kind of facial shape that was more attractive to the opposite sex and suggested blepharoplasty to open her eyes up and get rid of the fatty deposits on her eyelids. True to form these procedures were carried out together the following week and after convalescing for a month she was ready to meet up with her friends again; they hardly recognised her . . . she was looking fantastic.

But by now she was hooked . . . it was as easy to become addicted to this as it was to smoking crack. She wanted more . . . Ignatio suggested breast enhancement and a Brazilian Butt Lift.

He told her she would be his last surgery as he was retiring due to ill health (in fact he was dying of cancer).

So she had her last two operations when Ignatio gave her the breast size that most would envy and buttocks just like a Brazilian . . . large, firm and high, then she sadly bad him farewell.

Ignatio died that night with a smile on his face, one could say contented.

'Why?' You might ask. Because he had had his revenge.

Many years ago Ignatio's son had been slaughtered by a certain 'friend' of his in Colombia, a mafia baron called Jose Ortega. He had recognised Cecilia as he had known her as a child . . . in fact the two children has played together at the holiday resorts. And so he had hatched his little plan.

An eye for an eye.

As Cecilia had gained confidence so he was suggesting more radical surgeries until the finale . . . fireworks please!

At first Cecilia had been so pleased with her breasts and butt, but quite soon it became obvious that something was wrong.

Within days, as the polyurethane, slow expanding foam and formaldehyde mixture Ignatio had used as his filler expanded in her body, she had become housebound . . . she was hideous.

What was left of her body was found months later when the rental ran out . . . it plastered the walls . . . her skin had no longer been able to hold the expansion of the foam.

THE ZOO

Bryony

The animals were restless as though they sensed that something was amiss as they watched the owners of the zoo walking around the site that evening after it was closed. They were used to this happening but usually the owners stopped at most of the enclosures and talked to the occupants. So it was so unusual to see them walking round with no interaction talking quietly to each other with a serious look on their faces. What could be the matter? What had happened? The next day the animals woke to an eerie silence. Normally the voices of the keepers would rouse them but today it was too quiet. Instead of the keepers cleaning and feeding the animals in twos and threes – chatting together and talking to the different inmates – today there was only one keeper present on each section so it was taking longer to get their day areas cleaned and to be fed. At nine o'clock – when the gates usually clanged open and the human visitors started arriving – nothing happened and no one came. Usually the zoo was only closed to the public once a year on Christmas Day but it was now Spring. The animals were confused – but after a chain communication around the zoo no one was any the wiser.

'Let's ask The Professor what he thinks', suggested Mala, the matriarch of the elephant herd. The Professor was the zoo's oldest resident – a Galapagos giant tortoise who was rumoured to be well over a hundred years old.

'Well – the only time that I can remember the zoo being closed other than at Christmas was when there was a big storm many years ago and a lot of damage was done to the enclosures so the humans were afraid that some of us might escape', said The Professor. So that was no help as there had been no bad weather.

Nothing changed over the next few days although all the animals made a point of ensuring that they were awake and alert to see if the gates would open – but they remained shut. Then one day Korky, the African grey parrot, said that he had some news. Over the years he had learned more human words than most of the animals so he often eavesdropped on people's conversations. Mostly he heard things that were of no interest like what people were going to wear that night or what they were having for dinner – but today he had heard something new. He told the eagle, who told the chimpanzees, who told the elephants, and so on round the zoo – that he had heard that an illness had come to the world and because of that the humans were not allowed to be together outside their homes.

Korky had a friend from outside who visited from time to time – a herring gull – who lived in the City. So when he flew over a few days later Korky called out to him. He told Korky that times were hard outside as well as all the feeding stations that the humans used were shut and consequently all the bins that he used to forage in were empty and there were no discarded burger buns or takeaways on the pavement. He had been obliged to go fishing to feed himself which he found quite difficult as he was out of practice having lived on bin food for so long. He told Korky that most of the seagulls weren't going to breed this year as they were worried that there wouldn't be enough food for their chicks. Korky passed on the new information to the others through the zoo network.

The animals were perplexed and some of them became unnecessarily spiteful. The hyenas told the zebras and deer that if food ran out at the zoo the owners would be forced to feed them to the big cats and dog species. The lions licked their lips and the tigers flexed their claws wondering if they would get live fresh meat sometime soon! The evil rumour prompted a breeding frenzy in some species to ensure the continuation of their line should the worst befall and that caused other animals to do the same. The few keepers left to tend to the animals couldn't understand why wherever they looked the animals were mating.

'I don't know what's got into them', said the giraffe keeper, 'I haven't seen so much sexual activity in years. It will just end up with more mouths to feed which will cause us more problems'.

After a while things calmed down but the animals were getting very bored. Although they had sufficient to eat there wasn't the variety that they had previously enjoyed especially when some child dropped their lolly or other sweets into an enclosure by accident or design. And although it was refreshing not to have rude comments made by the humans (particularly the children) they missed making fun of the humans as well.

'I used to get fed up with the small ones pointing at my red bum and laughing', said Candy the alpha female Baboon, 'but I would welcome the diversion now. I used to turn round and wiggle it at them to mimic their walk which made me feel better'.

'And it was such fun to run up to the glass screen and thump it to make them jump and scream', said Grant the gorilla.

'And there was nothing better than using my trunk to squirt water at them', said Mala.

But one day the atmosphere changed. The keepers began working in pairs again although most of the animals agreed that they looked silly as they had *things* over their faces so you could only see their eyes. Later the animals were surprised to hear the gates open and to see a long line of visitors spaced out at intervals, and most of those were wearing *things* on their faces. Fences had been erected on the walkways between the enclosures so that there were one-way systems – both in and out – and the keepers were controlling the human movements so they were no longer allowed to get close to the enclosures or touch anything. The animals felt excited – it had been so quiet for the last few months. Mala started trumpeting followed by the rest of her family, the big cats roared, the monkeys and apes hooted, the birds called out loudly, the dogs howled and barked, and the zebras brayed. All the animals in the zoo contributed to the welcome. Then they performed to the best of their ability for the visitors. The keepers were amazed and the human visitors were overwhelmed. Unlike previously there were no rude comments about the animals but a strong appreciation for them and nature in general. So the animals concluded that although the shutdown of the zoo had been hard for them the end result appeared to be a change in attitude by the humans which acted in the best interests of everyone as it seemed to have made the world a better place.

'You should have seen us all performing for the humans', Korky told his seagull friend the next time he flew over, 'I have never seen the like before!'

A DAY IN THE LIFE

Mary

It is early, very early, the sky only just beginning to lighten with a pale wash of pink. I have just been through the wash my blue and chrome coat buffed and sparkling – looking good I say to myself and ready to face another day and meet my public. Several of us have drawn the short straw and have been chosen for the long shift from early until late – oh joy, another fun-filled day in paradise.

The huge doors open and our drivers wander in and what a motley crew they are, the usual miserable bunch. They all hate the early start. Personally I have never been able to understand their problem as they work a shorter shift, have a meal break then work another shift and go home – me I'm here until midnight and beyond. Good thing I don't need sleep.

My driver for the first part of the day is one of those people, who on the face of it, is charming to everyone. All I can say about that is it is just as well the people he meets don't hear his muttered less-than-complimentary comments when they are out of earshot. I rev my engine to drown him out, anything for a quiet life, this is a passenger-rage-free zone.

It takes him an age to get settled, first the seat is too high then too low, then too close to the steering wheel then too far away. The mirror isn't positioned correctly and so it goes on. At this rate we will be running late before we've even started. Yes I know this is all important for safety but I just want to get going. At last he switches on the engine and after a little reluctance on my part, I do like to let him know I'm in charge, we're off.

Our route today is from one of the outer city estates into the city centre then out over the river to another city estate on the other side, where we will turn round and do the whole thing in reverse all day, doing battle with mad drivers and lemming-like pedestrians who launch themselves into the road without looking, once one had stepped into the road the rest follow.

Our first passengers are the silent ones, the early workers plugged into their music. They don't acknowledge each other or my driver, the only sounds are muffled coughing and the bleep of the ticket machine as it reads season tickets and other passes. I look out for the little dark-haired girl, always late running for the bus, toast in hand. I don't see her today and wonder if she is even later than usual.

We stop at the hospital to disgorge the day shift and pick up some of those ending their night shift. It takes a few minutes for the exchange of passengers, some of whom are frantically taking the final drag on a cigarette before running for the door. My driver drives off leaving them behind which I think is rather mean. We speed through traffic lights as they change to red making no attempt to slow down. One day something will hit me and I'll have a big dent in my rather large derrière.

Now for the school run, endless shouting, screaming and swearing and that's just the mums. The little ones fall into two categories, those who want to go to school who are shouting and laughing, pushing each other to get on and off the bus and those who don't, some of whom are crying or are withdrawn dragging their feet and taking as long as they can to get on and off. The older students glued to their mobile phones not looking where they are going, how they don't trip I'll never know. Art students struggling with their portfolios, students with no bags at all, trying to outdo each other in the outrageous behaviour stakes.

We pull up at the stop outside the greengrocers and I see a little boy having a full-blown tantrum refusing to get on the bus, we have met him before several times and on each occasion he is having a tantrum. Mum tries to persuade him onto the bus but he isn't having any of it. With him kicking and screaming it probably isn't possible to carry him aboard. At last he is on the bus and the tantrum level goes up a notch, he is now lying on the floor in the aisle screaming. I can sense the passengers' unease as they stare pointedly at him hoping mum will take him off before we reach their stops. After what seems like an age but is really only three or four stops mother and child get off but not before going through the same scenario in reverse, he won't get off the bus. Some drivers less patient than mine have given up and driven off from the stop when he won't get on.

A change of driver now just in time for the older travellers. There is a little knot of them at every bus stop, making their way into the city centre or local shops, their entry accompanied by the bleep of the ticket machine reading passes or the angry growl when a pass cannot be read. On the whole they are a polite bunch, gossiping away about their neighbours, family members and other friends. It does take an age to get some of them settled with their walking frames and shopping trollies. We are very patient and wait for them all to be seated before moving off. Can't understand why some will insist on struggling to the back of the bus when there are seats at the front especially for the less mobile.

My new driver is a lovely lady who doesn't suffer fools gladly and can be a bit scary, the perfect attributes for this job. We are travelling out of town across the river over the bridge and through a busy suburb when we see a man in the middle of the road waving at us to stop. My driver sighs, we know this guy of old, he frightens other passengers. I hear my driver say, 'Oh no, you're not getting on my bus', and keeps going.

The day wears on and we trundle back and forth, back and forth picking up and depositing our cargo of noisy kids, happy shoppers, tired workers, cinemagoers, theatregoers and everyone else in between.

The pubs have closed now and I am coming up to my last journey of the day and my least favourite. Will our passengers be happy or aggressive, probably the usual mix of the two. Hopefully no one will be ill over my seats and I will not have to spend most of tomorrow being deep cleaned. I am pleasantly surprised, a rare final journey with no problems at all.

Tomorrow I'll be out there doing the same thing again. Another fun-filled day in paradise!

ONE SCAMMER'S PAYBACK

Lynda A

Boredom hit badly during the second Covid lockdown; the first had been bearable as the weather was so beautiful and encouraged me to walk in nature every day. The second lockdown was in the winter, it was cold, grey and wet; who wants to go out in that unless they have to.

As a result of my ennui I decided to take a look at online dating along with quite a high percentage of the population. I didn't want a toyboy (been there, done that, and have the worn-out T-shirt), I wanted someone closer to my age with a similar background and interests.

The first few men who communicated with me were either too young or very unattractive (both physically and in their profiles). Then I was contacted by Geoff, he looked attractive and his profile sounded interesting, so I replied to his email. We mailed back and forth for a couple of weeks before he suggested we meet up for a picnic which he offered to provide.

We met on The Common the following day, which was luckily dry and not so cold, and walked together to one of the picnic benches. The picnic he had brought was a better quality than I had expected mostly Marks and Spencer's prepacked salads (all sealed) with wooden forks. We sat and ate whilst chatting, he was easy company and the whole thing was absolutely perfect for our first date. He not only talked about his past life but also asked about mine which, in my experience, is quite unusual. He was taller than me, had quite a good head of hair, and was quite attractive . . . very much like his profile photo.

Once we had finished eating we walked a little more and agreed that we would both like to meet again and also continue our contact by email.

Our conversations continued on a daily basis and I found it a relief and pleasure to open my Hotmail account every morning and receive an update from a person rather than just the usual offers from Groupon and frightening Covid death rates etc. from *The Guardian*. We also had a couple more pleasant dates on the Common or in the city parks.

Then I suddenly started receiving emails from friends asking why I had sent them somewhat worrying emails, which I knew I hadn't sent; I also had subjects posted on my Facebook account which I hadn't posted myself . . . right-wing propaganda and other, rather hateful subjects; people I had known for years stopped my contact and removed themselves from my friends list . . . understandably.

I also started receiving phone calls from people unknown to me, people who greeted me as if I was a very close friend . . . I began to feel vulnerable in my own home. What was going on? How was this all possible? I was feeling more isolated by the day, and more dependent on my daily emails from my new friend . . . the one I was beginning to feel I could count on to be there for me.

I sat in the bath one evening with a glass of wine to try to sort out when exactly this had all started; I always do my best thinking when relaxing in hot water.

Nothing like this had happened before . . . before what? Actually, I realised, before I had met Geoff. Although he had told me that he was a bit of a technophobe, he could have been lying; it made sense looking at the timeframe.

I went to the local library to do a bit of research, this may sound a bit neurotic but I was now assuming that Geoff had some sort of access to my computer . . . somebody did.

A week later I phoned Geoff and suggested that we meet on The Common again and that this time I would bring the picnic, it was my turn.

We met at our usual spot and had a gentle stroll through the beautiful nature that is The Common and then made our way to our picnic bench. I set out the egg mayo and chicken with pickle sandwiches, vegetable samosas and lemon drizzle cake that I had made especially for the occasion; by this time I was feeling quite peckish.

Being a vegetarian I went straight into the egg mayo sandwiches, being a meat eater Geoff started on the chicken; we both enjoyed some samosas and cake washed down with coffee from my flask.

We were chatting away, as before, when he mentioned that he was having severe financial problems and wouldn't be able to pay his rent that month . . . he was terrified of being homeless which was quite understandable. I asked him for his bank details promising to transfer enough to pay his rent for the month on the understanding that he would sort out his finances however he could.

I started packing up what was left of the picnic ready to go home; I noticed, with pleasure, that he had eaten all the chicken sandwiches that I had prepared just for him along with several samosas and slices of cake . . . he had a good appetite.

I told him that I was going home to get started on my transfer; he said he wasn't feeling too good so would sit there for a while until he felt better. We agreed that we would email each other again the following day and I left him sitting in the sun.

The following day I noticed in our local news that an elderly man had been found dead on The Common of unknown causes but that foul play was not suspected; it was assumed that, due to his age, he had suffered a huge heart attack.

A new programme started on TV that a friend had suggested I watch about how unscrupulous people were profiting from others' loneliness during the pandemic by joining dating sites and befriending those who were feeling isolated. They showed how these corrupt, ruthless people had managed to worm their way into their unsuspecting victims' lives and obtain money from them . . . in some cases they had even persuaded their prey to send them money to help them leave a country where they were being held hostage, in one case a woman was convinced to sell her house so they could buy a new one together.

And there was Geoff . . . he was one of the shady, immoral characters who had profited from more than one woman.

It did make me feel better that, thanks to my research in the library and a quick trip to the New Forest to pick mushrooms (those red ones with white spots that always look like something out of a fairy story), I had managed to rid the world of one pervert.

FALLING

Bryony

I was falling and I was terrified. The air was rushing past me and I felt helpless as there was nothing I could do to stop myself. What was going to happen to me – would I ever be found? Had I been a fool to decide on a walking holiday on my own just to prove that I could against the wishes of my family who thought I was having a senior moment? Finally my fall came to an abrupt stop as I found myself at the edge of thicket of bushes which had prevented me rolling any further down the hill. I took stock and gingerly moved all my limbs and generally checked myself for injuries. It seemed as if I had been lucky although I might have a few bruises tomorrow. But where was I?

If I had continued following the path which had given way under me I would have eventually come to a village which had been my destination for the night. But now I was hopelessly lost. I looked around me for landmarks or signs of life but I couldn't see anything. I gingerly stood up keeping hold of the branches and then I saw the house. It was in a dip and would not have been visible from the path due to the trees and bushes around it. It was a two storey dwelling with what looked like a small hedged garden and a large upper terrace. However it had obviously been empty for some considerable time as it was overgrown with ivy and there was no glass in many of the windows. But I reasoned that if I could make my way down to it there should be a path leading from there to the village which would have been used for access when it was occupied. But this was easier said than done as the descent was steep.

I slowly and carefully edged my way downwards moving from tree to tree and bush to bush to ensure that I had something to hold onto. I had to take a wide circular route as to travel down from where I had first seen the house would have been impossible as it was almost vertical. After what seemed forever I eventually made it to the lower ground but I could not see the house anymore. Had I imagined it? I decided to stop to rest and take stock, and after a drink of water and a biscuit bar I felt better and continued my search. I was about to give up and try and find my way back up to the original path when I suddenly came upon it in the opposite direction from where I had searched previously.

The dwelling was even more deserted and rundown than it had seemed from my first sight of it. I walked around it pushing my way past and through shrubs and bushes that had claimed the land around it. Eventually I came to what appeared to be the entrance. Should I go in? My sensible voice said, 'no', as I didn't know whether it was safe but curiosity overcame my reservations and I pushed the decaying wooden door. It was stiff but after a bit of effort it moved to reveal that the first room had been invaded by almost as much vegetation as was outside. The house must have been abandoned for years. Just as I was considering whether to proceed further the heavens opened so unless I wanted to get soaked I had no option but to seek shelter inside. As I looked up I could see that the ceiling was occupied by various birds and in the corner a colony of bats who had created a mound of smelly guano in one corner. I am not fond of these winged rodents so I kept well away from that area. The birds were not pleased with my presence as they were all squawking loudly to warn of possible danger. In the opposite corner to the bat area I noticed that there was a stone stairway so I made my way towards it and cautiously moved upwards a step at a time. It led to a small vestibule with two doors.

I opened the first door which led out onto the terrace that I had seen earlier but as it was now raining heavily I did not proceed further. The second door led to further stairs which I ascended as cautiously as the first. But the door at the top was not easily opened as it must have swelled with damp and lack of use. I needed to see if there was anywhere beyond that would offer better shelter for the night as the storm had shortened the day and I would be unable to progress further in the darkness. I was beginning to resign myself to spending the night in the vestibule as I did not relish sharing the night with the bats when I wondered if I could break a hole in the door with a rock as it was so rotten. I made my way back down and halfway I came across a large stone that must have fallen in from the walls. I started attacking the door and easily managed to create a large hole. When I looked through I could see in the fading light that this room looked dry as it only had one window which was still partially glazed and didn't appear to have so much outside occupation as downstairs. I continued to break wood from the door until I could crawl through.

It was getting darker all the time and although there was no signal on my phone I was able to use it to make my way across the room. But I had to be careful not to run down the battery as I had not topped up the charge before setting out that morning. I drank some more water and had another biscuit bar before making myself as comfortable as possible in the area away from the open window. I was too tired to worry about what might be in the room with me as the exertion of the climb down and breaking the door must have exhausted me and I quickly fell asleep. The next thing I knew was that it was morning and I woke up feeling stiff. I was also hot as I had put on my extra jumper and my waterproof to protect me from the night chill but the sun was now heating up the room through the window. I still had half a bottle of water but although I felt very thirsty I rationed myself to a few sips as I didn't know when I would be able to find more and I ate my last biscuit bar. I was about to set out when I noticed another door in the corner of the room. Someone had originally pushed a wardrobe in front of it but over the years it had rotted to reveal the outline of the door. Should I take a look – why not otherwise I would always wonder what was on the other side.

The carcass of the wardrobe moved easily and the door opened without problem. Inside there was a bed, a child's cradle and a large chest. Cobwebs were everywhere hanging like grey and black curtains so I found a stick to move them away before proceeding further. I moved towards the chest but then I glanced at the bed and was horrified to see that resting on the disintegrating mattress were two skeletons. I could tell from what was left of the clothing of the larger one that it was that of a woman and I presumed that cradled in her arms was her child. Had someone deliberately concealed their bodies by moving the wardrobe in front of the door? I retraced my steps through the house and once outside I was able to locate a path which I followed to a local road. Here I could get a phone signal so immediately rang the police to report my discovery. I never found out who they were or what might have happened as after taking my statement the authorities needed no more from me and said that I was free to continue my holiday. But at least I knew that they would now be laid to rest rather than being left to turn to dust in the abandoned ruin.

THE DIARY

Mary

Maureen had always kept a diary starting from early childhood when it contained notes of her everyday life in a rural setting. Life was fun and this was reflected in the entries which were interspersed with her sketches, pictures and cuttings from the local weekly newspaper of school plays, sports days, exam results, Brownies and Guide camps. As she grew into her teenage years all her crushes and love affairs, mostly imagined, were recorded there. The sketches and newspaper cuttings giving way to cinema and theatre tickets, guide books and entrance tickets to some of Europe's most popular tourist destinations.

Maureen left home in her twenties and moved to the city for work. Although life was hectic with a pressurised job and busy, busy social life her attention to her diary didn't waver as it had been part of her daily routine for so many years. The diary now contained paragraphs about life in the office, her dislike of a colleague, friends and family weddings, births and deaths. Theatre trips were still a much-loved activity the diary bursting with tickets and programmes.

When Maureen met Ray her diary entries went into overdrive. He was the love of her life and her diary reflected this as it was dedicated almost exclusively to him in the early years of their relationship and subsequent marriage. Following the birth of their two daughters Ray took a back seat as the girls' lives took over the entries, birthdays, first days at school, nativity plays, family celebrations and bereavements together with all the minutiae of life in a busy home.

The years passed so quickly, the girls went out into the world and her beloved husband died suddenly and unexpectedly.

When Ray died it was as if the liferaft that kept her afloat had deflated and Maureen was left drifting and floundering in the sea that was life.

Now Maureen herself was facing the twilight of her life. She worried about her daughters as she had always done. The elder one who just didn't conform hiding behind a façade as hard as nails, didn't need anyone and so independent. It was just an act, underneath that tough image she was as soft as marshmallow. Would she face a lonely old age as she had never married and had no family Maureen worried.

Her younger daughter happily married and a grandmother herself now had overcome a long battle with an eating disorder and seemed content with life.

Her diary was by her bed in the quiet room with its muted peaceful décor, a room that could be in any smart hotel anywhere only the regular visits by the nurses pointing to the fact that it wasn't. A vase containing her favourite Graham Thomas roses stood on a small table by the window, their deep yellowy-orange petals the colour of the midday sun. Maureen knew that she didn't have long since the brutal diagnosis two months earlier. She so desperately wanted to write her final thoughts in her diary but she had no strength to hold the pen and marshalling her thoughts was becoming harder as with the passing days the pain became impossible to bear, the drugs needed to alleviate it stronger. The diary remained unopened.

This cruel disease which affected not only her but all those around her, her beloved family and such dear supportive friends. She wanted to tell that she wasn't afraid of leaving this world as she believed that what she was going into would be better, she was leaving the pain, leaving the feeling induced by the morphine and she would see her beloved Ray again also her parents and a beautiful grandson taken at such a young age.

The diary remained unopened to be found by her daughters two days later. When it was opened they could both hear their mother's voice:

My beautiful daughters I am so sorry I won't be with you to see you through life. I know I didn't say this often enough but I love you dearly and I am so very proud of you both and everything you have achieved. I am so proud of my tall strong grandsons who have enriched my life beyond words. You have made your way in the world against so many difficulties and I love you. My wonderful great grandson I regret that I will not see you grow and become that firefighter you always told me you were going to be.

My special beloved family and my wonderful friends, please don't mourn too long for me. Remember life is there to be lived so go out and grab it by the horns and do just that.

DOORS

Lynda A

Most people over the age of forty have probably heard of the Magic Faraway Tree situated in the Enchanted Wood. It was inhabited by what were termed as 'queer folk', which, back in the day was not considered politically incorrect and meant peculiar, unusual people; people with strange names like Moon-Face, Silky, Dame Washalot, Mr Whatsisname and The Saucepan Man.

Even more magical was the fact that bizarre lands would arrive at the cloud at the top of the tree; lands which stayed for a while and which, if you visited the land, you had to make sure you left before the land itself did or you could find yourself living in that land . . . possibly forever. If that land happened to be *The Land of Take What You Want* or *The Land of Birthdays* that could have been pleasant; but if it was one like *The Land of the Red Goblins* you just had to steer clear as they would take you prisoner.

What very few people know is that there is another tree in that forest; unlike the Faraway Tree it is not visited by children; the inhabitants, although they could also be termed 'queer folk', are not, on the whole, as welcoming as the residents of that magical tree.

The first door in the other tree is quite rustic looking; it has roses around the door and part of the forest floor has been cleared to make a flower garden close to the tree and an allotment nearby . . . this one looks inviting.

If you accept this visual invitation, and knock, the door will be opened by a smiling, somewhat scruffy man; the kind of man who enjoys growing fruit and veg and makes his own jam.

He will probably be happy to see you; if it's raining he will invite you inside and feed you coffee or tea with homemade cakes sitting by a roaring fire . . . he will even give you the best chair. If the sun is shining you will be treated to the same hospitality in his beautiful, well-tended garden. With him you will be able to have an interesting conversation and truly put the world to rights with less criticism and more empathy; when you leave him you know you will visit again as you will depart feeling uplifted, with a more positive outlook on the world.

The second door is blue and very shiny, but getting a little rough around the edges; obviously the occupant started off his residence with high hopes for the future but had little idea of how to look after anything . . . this can be seen by the fact that the edging of the door is becoming rotten and there are lots of cobwebs filled with poor victims that the spider never got round to eating. Although originally this door might have looked attractive and welcoming, that is no longer the case.

If you knock on this door expect to wait a little. If you knock on this door it will be eventually opened a crack by a scruffy, tow-headed man. Do not expect a smile straight away as the occupant is very wary, with god reason. He will want to know how you vote and your opinion of his governing of your country.

If you vote Conservative and tell him you felt he had done a good job whilst in power he may invite you in for a beer . . . if you vote Labour and want to ask him questions about his cronyism whilst in office, about his continual U-turns, about all the money he wasted making poor decisions he will definitely not let you in. He will try to shut the door in your face. Should you have put your foot in the doorway to stop it shutting he will disappear straight away into a large fridge just inside the door and not come out again until you have left and the coast is clear.

When you leave him you know that you will never, ever return again . . . why would you?

The third door is larger than the others; it is red with gold accoutrements, lots of gold accoutrements. To call it gaudy would be an understatement. It's the kind of door that would appeal to people with little taste but who would like to be more upward mobile, people who would be equally showily materialistic given the chance.

Your wait at this door will be even longer as the inhabitant has to make sure his hair is looking as full as possible and that every hair is in the correct comb-over position; he must also apply a quick layer of tan make-up.

When you realise who lives there you will be inclined to carry on with your climb up the tree in the knowledge that the likelihood of a true conversation is verging on nil; if you enjoy being talked at with a content of three letter words then you are in for a treat. Better to continue with your journey and possibly send off a tweet.

The fourth door is also large, very large in fact and also red. Within this large door there is a smaller door which appears more used than the containing monstrosity.

Again, expect a wait if you knock on this door as the occupier will have to put some secret wedges into his shoes before answering . . . he is short for someone who is/was a leader of men; someone who has always appeared as large as his cohorts and twice as healthy and manly.

He may be preceded to the door by some poorly-trained dogs and he will probably not have a shirt on as, in all possibility, he will have been training his upper body. If you are not tall he might well invite you into his abode; if he is eating breakfast he may well share his quails eggs with you and offer a coffee.

I have no idea how your conversation with this man will go; I would imagine he would be opinionated and quite a hard man.

The final door, near the top of the tree, appears more like a lift door. It is made of metal and has no accessories at all. You originally think there is no way to alert the occupant that someone is at his door until you notice a tiny camera following your every move. Evidently someone very powerful, but also very guarded and cagey, lives in this penthouse.

You will not be invited into this abode. Every move you make is being watched to discern your reason for being there, to perceive whether or not you are a threat . . . whether or not to shoot you. This is the only dwelling that has access to the Slippery Slip . . . the chute inside the tree, which goes round and round the core, exiting at the back of the tree through a hatch which is shielded from view by a large bush. The hatch is remote-controlled to stop people gaining access to his penthouse (in what would be an incredibly taxing manner) by climbing up the Slippery Slip.

Pablo Escobar is the resident of the penthouse . . . the one who has most to fear from mafia rivals, hence all the exterior protection. He has been reported as deceased but that was just to protect him, to save his life while he escaped from Medellin. Because he likes unpredictable weather he was flown, by private jet, to England and here he stays.

I had to include his door because, when we lived in Colombia, if we went to any upmarket blocks of flats we would press the buttons for every floor to see how many were mafia . . . you could always tell when the lift door opened; mostly the mafia apartments had another sheet metal door so you couldn't even leave the lift. This was back in 1986 when the mafia was very strong in Colombia, many said that the government was owned by them at the time.

I'm sure you can guess who the other occupants were.

THROUGH THE WINDOW

Bryony

I had made my way into the garden by climbing over a high red-brick wall covered in dense ivy that provided useful footholds as the stems were thick and wiry. I slowly crept past clipped evergreen shrubs and along by the edge of the well-tended lawn until I was near to the house which stood alone in the large grounds. Most of the house was in darkness but I could see that a light shone through the curtains in a downstairs room so I made my way forward to see if I could find out who was at home. The curtains had slightly gaped a little at the side as if pulled across too hastily, and I looked into the room.

I could see a copper-based lamp with a multi-coloured glass shade close to the window that I was peering through standing on a dresser with two pottery birds beside it. The colours of the lampshade reflected on the birds which would have looked dull without the many colours of the glass randomly lighting up their surfaces. Beside the dresser there was a large winged armchair with a cracked and worn leather covering. It had once been a deep shade of red but now had a mottled appearance which looked like a desert with scorched-earth patterns imprinted on it. Here and there were patches that had not been so badly abused that shone a dull but faded red plum.

In the chair sat a woman who was reading what appeared to be a long letter. She was holding one page in her hand and there were other pages on her lap. She was an elegant woman of mature years. Her hair, now grey with distinctive streaks of white, was piled high on her head in a loose sort of bun and kept in place by a multitude of pins. Some of it had come loose and hung at the back of her neck in tendrils, and there was a piece at the front that she kept pushing back in an exasperated manner when it fell forward as she was reading. I got the impression that her sight was failing somewhat as she held the letter close to her face despite wearing gold-rimmed spectacles that were perched low on her nose. She must have been a great beauty when she was younger as she was still very attractive now despite her years. She had high cheekbones and a full mouth albeit now set between two deep lines that ran down from the side of her nose to the beginning of her chin. Her eyebrows were well-shaped, and her eyes shone a dark shade of violet with many laughter lines fanning out beside them like the rays of the sun. She was wearing long gold earrings which were set with a green stone that caught the light from the lamp as she moved.

As she was reading she was smiling so the contents of the letter obviously pleased her. Once or twice she seemed to laugh although I was unable to hear whether this was out loud or silently, being outside the window. Having finished one page she picked up another but her face suddenly appeared to grow stern and angry as she moved down the page. Then all of a sudden she stood up and the pages fell to the floor. She looked distraught and placed her hands over her face. I noticed how well manicured her nails were – shaped and painted a deep red in sharp contrast to the blue veins that stood out on the back of her hands. She was wearing a single ring on her left hand that looked out of place as it was a large and masculine sovereign ring. She stamped her feet in frustration and walked towards a cabinet. As she opened the door I could see that it contained glasses and bottles and she poured herself a large brandy which she downed in one gulp. I wished that I could join her as the cold was beginning to bite.

She returned to the chair and picked up the fallen pages that had been scattered in her distress. Putting them back in order she returned again to the page that had upset her. She scanned it again and then started shaking her head. She was mouthing words that I could not hear but I could see by the set of her mouth, and the way that her eyebrows were raised and eyes half closed that she was not pleased with the content. She continued to read the rest of the letter quickly then re-read the last pages as if she was hoping to find better news.

She stood up again. A tall, slim woman with an erect posture wearing a dark green dress of what looked like a velvet material with a high neck with long sleeves that had a tight cuff. A gold necklace with a single green-stoned pendant matched her earrings. Another large brandy was drunk and then she started to pace the floor. As she turned to walk towards the window she seemed to look straight at me so I ducked down below the windowsill but when I looked again she had turned and was walking down the room away from me. She was obviously thinking out loud as her face contorted from time to time and her lips moved frequently. All of a sudden she stopped and moved over to a writing desk in the corner of the room. She took out pen and paper and started furiously writing – I imagined that it was a reply to the letter that had disturbed her or maybe a note to someone else to inform them what she had learned. The letter did not take long to write and she had soon addressed it and affixed a stamp, leaving it on the desk to post.

The woman then returned to the armchair and curled up in a foetal position. Then she wept. Tears coursed down her face like a never-ending waterfall and her body shook with violent tremors. I felt as if I should comfort her but I could not do so from outside the window.

I stood up and turned away as I felt that I could no longer intrude. I am not usually a sentimental person and I had intended to break in to the house to steal what I could – but the scene that I had witnessed had moved me greatly so I could not find it in my heart to add to the woman's distress. I scaled the wall again and went on my way in search of another likely target.

THE CLOCK STOPPED

Mary

There was a builder's skip outside number 43, its once bright sunshine-yellow coating faded now after years of exposure to the elements, tracks of rust gouged out of its sides. It looked out of place on that street of tidy terraced houses as if it had been dropped by a gigantic bird as it flew overhead no longer able to manage the weight.

A man stood by the skip, nondescript-looking, neither old nor young, tall nor short, a knitted-hat pulled low over his eyes. The house was being cleared and as each box, drawer or item of furniture was brought out the man checked the item, some of which were placed carefully to one side the rest tossed contemptuously into the skip.

It was with some sadness that Elaine and her husband Chris watched from the front bedroom window of their house opposite. They had both been brought up on this street and never wanted to move away so when the opportunity to buy their house arose they took it and all those years later were still there.

Number 43 had been home to William and Maisie Evans who had moved in as young newlyweds. Unable to have children of their own they quickly became known as Uncle Billy and Auntie Maisie to most of the local children over time including Elaine, Chris and their children. Uncle Billy and Auntie Maisie loved children, they were always ready to babysit, look after the little ones after school and during the school holidays. Uncle Billy had a wonderful model railway in a shed at the bottom of the garden and in a time when life was simpler the children loved it. Auntie Maisie made the most amazing cakes, wonderful feather-light sponges with soft fluffy buttercream fillings topped with hundreds and thousands or chocolate sprinkles. Elaine could still remember sitting in the kitchen at number 43 on a stool when she was young and her feet didn't reach the ground when Auntie Maisie would lift her up with her usual cheerful, 'up you come'. The kitchen would always smell wonderful, full of the aromas of baking or freshly-ironed linen.

But now number 43 looked unloved and neglected, no one left to care for it, keep the garden tidy, the grass cut and the shrubs trimmed. A property developer had snapped up the house and contents when they came up for auction recently and now his workman were making their mark accompanied by a radio blaring out loud music which was unbearable for the immediate neighbours.

The house had been empty for some time. Elaine was at home the day the ambulance arrived in the road, blue lights flashing, sirens screaming. Uncle Billy had had a heart attack. The paramedics were there for what seemed like an age before taking him to hospital where, despite the best care, he died a few days later.

It was a measure of the fondness and respect everyone had for him that virtually the whole street, not to mention those who had moved away over the years, attended his funeral at the local crematorium where those who were unable to find a seat stood around the walls and outside the door.

Auntie Maisie was devastated, her reason for living snatched away. Elaine and Chris brought her to stay with them but she couldn't settle and after a week or so returned home. The neighbours rallied round, they took her shopping, invited her for dinner, organised the garden and arranged for the model railway to be sold as Maisie just couldn't bear to see it just left.

Time passed oh, so quickly on silent wings, Maisie stayed in the house for as long as possible until it was obvious to everyone that she just wasn't able to care for herself even with the help of neighbours and carers. It was a sad day when she too was taken into hospital and then into care and a month later passed away peacefully in her sleep.

A day or so after the arrival of the skip Elaine was walking home from the shops and passed the now full skip outside number 43. It was horrible to see all Uncle Billy and Auntie Maisie's much loved possessions tossed aside as rubbish. The property developers had arranged for someone to go through the contents of the house and that was the man in the woollen hat, anything with any monetary value had gone to be sold. Elaine stopped by the skip, she couldn't explain it but she felt she wanted something tangible to go with the memories of childhood so much of which was spent in that house. Something held her back, hadn't there been an incident where a member of the public had been prosecuted for removing something from a skip on the roadside? But who owned this pile of rubbish, the property developer who bought the house and contents perhaps but would he care? It had no value for him and was destined for landfill.

Elaine cast her eye over the contents so much of which was broken. The she saw it, the cream alarm clock, one of the old-fashioned wind-up type with two large bells on the top. She smiled as she remembered this being on the mantelpiece in the lounge which she always thought was strange as in her home the alarm clock lived in the bedroom. Even though she couldn't remember why the alarm had been set she could remember how the vibration from it would cause the clock to walk to the edge of the mantelpiece where Uncle Billy would catch it before it fell into the hearth.

She reached into the skip to retrieve the clock and noticed that it had stopped at 3:35. She knew it was fanciful but she was sure that it was around that time Auntie Maisie had left the house for the last time.

The clock now lives in the kitchen in Elaine's home, it still shows 3:35 and no amount of cleaning and coaxing will make it go.

THE UNPAID BILL

Bryony

Many years ago I had agreed to be one of the executors to my cousin's will. I had not thought much about it at the time as there were two other executors named but they were now deceased so I was left with the sole responsibility. What a daunting task – so much to do – which was not made any easier by the fact that I lived in London and she had lived in a village in Suffolk. So there was no other option but to take leave from work – just as well that I had holiday time owing – and make my way to Suffolk.

I must confess that there had been little contact between us for years other than the annual Christmas card. The last time that I saw her was about six years before her passing at the 21st birthday party of another cousin's daughter. I had always thought her strange when we were young but at the party I found her quite eccentric and unsettling and any attempts on my part to resume contact were rebuffed. Indeed I had wondered why she had attended the celebration as she kept herself isolated and spoke very little. She had left early driving away in a rather nice red sports car that did not match her generally staid and old fashioned appearance. However I was sorry to hear that she had been killed in a car accident so near to her cottage.

I had been contacted by her solicitor who informed me of her demise as apparently she had named me as next of kin and I had arranged to meet with him after I had settled myself into my hotel. The will was pretty straightforward as the only beneficiaries were two charities. My cousin's death had been registered and her funeral had already been arranged as she had a paid up plan and had left specific instructions with her solicitor – cremation with no attendees and no service. But I needed to sort out the cottage and he passed me a sealed envelope addressed to 'Executor' which contained the key to the cottage and a slip of paper on which was written, 'Mother's DOB plus house number', which did not make any sense to me.

The next day I drove to the cottage. It was in a fairly remote location and if I had not been given detailed instructions I would not have found it. Surprisingly it looked well-kept from the outside and similarly so inside. The furniture looked expensive and the place was neat and tidy apart from some washing up left in the sink. At the end of the kitchen was a door that led to a study which looked equally well organised so this was where I decided to make a start. The solicitor had told me that I needed to provide him with information about utility suppliers, bank accounts etc. so that everyone could be informed as debtors and creditors had to be established for the estate. As everything was so well-organised in filing cabinets with appropriate labelling this was a relatively easy task so I just had to place the paperwork it in the boxes that had kindly been provided by the solicitor.

I thought that I had finished in that room and was preparing to stop for lunch and then to start on the rest of the place when I noticed a locked cash box at the back of the bottom drawer of the cabinet. But where was the key? I thought that it might contain cash and jewellery which would need to be declared. Not in the desk drawer which contained only paper and envelopes. Then I moved to the bedroom but there was no key in the bedside table drawers or anywhere else that thought that someone might hide a key. Before searching further I rang the solicitor as I wondered if the cash box key might have been with the keys retrieved from the car after the accident. He said that nothing had been passed to him but that he would ring the hospital to find out whether my cousin's personal effects from the car had been retained by them for collection and later he told me that he had collected a set of keys and her handbag. I continued with my clearing – stacking items and clothes into separate areas for charity shops or to sell and was surprised when the solicitor appeared with the keys as I had planned to pick them up the next day. Sure enough there was a likely key and I was pleased to see that it fitted the box which contained an invoice for £7000 to be paid in cash to 'The Gardener' attached to the bundle. Although the garden of the cottage was well maintained I could not imagine what had been done for that amount. I gave the cash to the solicitor for which he gave me a receipt but I kept the invoice to see if I could locate the gardener's details so I could make contact and pay him. Perhaps the neighbours or someone in the village might know who he was as there were no details on the invoice.

The next day I started on my cousin's kitchen. I was clearing the larder of canned food and any dried foods that were unopened to take to the Food Bank when I noticed that at the back behind a screen there was what appeared to be a safe. It was locked of course – but what was the combination. I remembered the slip of paper that had been in the envelope with cottage key, 'My mother's DOB' would have been my aunt who had died some years earlier but I did not know her house number or birthday – but my mum might have the information. I rang several times before she answered the phone but eventually after a long rambling discussion she came up with the date of birth and possibly the house number where her sister had lived since her marriage until she passed. A longshot but it was worth a try. I turned the dial and the safe opened and inside was a notebook and another sealed letter. The note inside the envelope read as follows:

If you are reading this I will not be around to pay the price. You may have wondered how I made a living? I arrange for people to be despatched on request. Some were husbands or wives who were cheating; some were those who had ruined the lives of others; some were thieves or blackmailers; some were just evil and there were some about whom I was never told. I have a network of despatchers who are available for a fee according to what is required. I call them from a payphone and agree the terms and they are always paid in cash left in an agreed location. The notebook contains details of those who

149

were despatched and when but not by whom. There is no good reason for me to have kept this record other than my vanity as who would ever guess that I was capable of arranging these events. But how people get in touch with me to book a despatch or how my operatives inform me of their success is something that will be never be revealed. To compensate for my life of arranging deaths I have left all my money to charities helping the abused. I have no regrets as it was my choice to rid the world of those who deserved it.

I was stunned! I looked at the notebook and saw that the date of the latest despatch was only two days before her car crash! On the advice of the solicitor I passed the notebook to the police who confirmed that all those named over a period of almost twenty-three years had indeed been murdered or recorded as missing. I thought about the cash that I had passed to the solicitor and assumed that it had been for 'despatch services rendered'. But that is a bill that will remain unpaid.

Printed in Great Britain
by Amazon